PENGUIN BOOKS

The Tulip Touch

ANNE FINE was born and educated in the Midlands, and now lives in County Durham. She has written numerous highly acclaimed and prize-winning books for children and adults.

The Tulip Touch won the Whitbread Children's Book of the Year Award; *Goggle-Eyes* won the *Guardian* Children's Fiction Award and the Carnegie Medal, and was adapted for television by the BBC; *Flour Babies* won the Carnegie Medal and the Whitbread Children's Book Award; *Bill's New Frock* won a Smarties Prize; and *Madame Doubtfire* inspired the highly successful film *Mrs Doubtfire*.

Anne Fine was named Children's Laureate in 2001. She received an OBE in 2003, and was elected as a Fellow of the Royal Society of Literature. Anne's work has now been translated into forty-five languages.

Books by Ann Fine

BILL'S NEW FROCK

BLOOD FAMILY

BLUE MOON DAY

THE BOOK OF THE BANSHEE

THE CHICKEN GAVE IT TO ME

CRUMMY MUMMY AND ME

HOW TO WRITE REALLY BADLY

GOGGLE-EYES

STEP BY WICKED STEP

THE ROAD OF BONES

UP ON CLOUD NINE

The Tulip Touch

Anne Fine

PENGUIN BOOKS

PENGUIN BOOKS

UK | USA | Canada | Ireland | Australia
India | New Zealand | South Africa

Penguin Books is part of the Penguin Random House group of companies
whose addresses can be found at global.penguinrandomhouse.com.

www.penguin.co.uk
www.puffin.co.uk
www.ladybird.co.uk

Penguin
Random House
UK

First published by Hamish Hamilton Ltd 1996
Published by Puffin Books 1997
This edition published 2018

001

Set in 12.2/18 pt Dante MT Std
Typeset by Jouve (UK) Milton Keynes
Printed in Great Britain by Clays Ltd, St Ives plc

A CIP catalogue record for this book is available from the British Library

ISBN: 978-0-241-331194

All correspondence to:
Penguin Books
Penguin Random House Children's
80 Strand, London WC2R ORL

MIX
Paper from
responsible sources
FSC® C018179

Penguin Random House is committed to a
sustainable future for our business, our readers
and our planet. This book is made from Forest
Stewardship Council® certified paper.

Part One

I

You shouldn't tell a story till it's over, and I'm not sure this one is. I'm not even certain when it really began, unless it was the morning Dad thrust my bawling brother Julius back in Mum's arms, and picked up the ringing telephone.

'The Palace? Why ever would they want me at the Palace?'

Anyone listening might have begun to think of royal garden parties, or something. But even back then, when I heard people saying things like 'the black horse' or 'the palace', I got a different picture. And that's because I've lived in hotels all my life. I don't even remember the first one, the Old Ship. Mum says it was small and ivy-covered, with only six bedrooms. Then Dad was manager of the North Bay. And later he was moved to the Queen's Arms, where we were living then.

'So what's the Palace's problem?'

3

He listened so long, and sighed so heavily, that Mum had looked up from trying to placate Julius with his favourite furry rabbit even before we heard Dad say,

'And I suppose you've forgotten I already have thirty beds to run here, not to mention a small son who makes sure nobody can even *think*.'

That's when he noticed us watching, and, turning his back, finished almost in a whisper.

'All right. I'll drive over. Just to take a look.'

I don't know what time he got back, but it was late. Our flat was above the kitchens, and the huge extractor fans had stopped humming. The only sounds left were the usual muffled telephones and scurrying footsteps.

At breakfast, he said to me:

'You ought to see it, Natalie. It's enormous. It's got over sixty bedrooms, and it sits on its lawns like a giant great wedding cake set out on a perfect green tablecloth.'

'When can we come?'

He glanced at Mum, worn out from another bad night with Julius.

'Soon. Before I finish there. I'll take you over for the day.'

But when we finally saw it, it wasn't for the day. It was with suitcases and boxes and bags.

'I'm sorry about this,' Dad kept saying. 'I really did think this was going to be a short job.'

4

Mum tried to resettle Julius in the hot crush of his car seat. He squawked and struggled. And, tense from the packing, she complained the whole way.

'A few lumps of plaster falling in the guests' hair, you told me. Three weeks at most, till all the ceilings were fixed. And now it's wet rot. And dry rot. And problems with the piping, and the fire doors. Why can't the old manager cope? He's the one who let it all happen.'

Dad knew there was no point in answering. He just drove.

'One man not up to his job,' Mum grumbled. 'And suddenly three weeks is three months, and Natalie has to come out of school a week before the holidays, and –'

We swung round the last bend, and she broke off. Before us stood the Palace, vast and imposing, silencing petty complaints.

Dad switched off the engine and Mum scrambled out. Julius immediately stopped struggling and fell quiet. Mum unstrapped him and lifted him into her arms. And as she carried him up the wide stone steps to the Palace, suddenly behind her the whole sky was ablaze. And on the lawns on either side of her, the peacocks spread their glimmering fans.

'See?' Dad whispered to me, triumphant. 'A good omen!'

But I felt differently. I felt so strange. I think I must have

5

been dizzy from the ride. I stumbled out of the car, and suddenly the sky seemed too high above me, the grass too green. And then one of the peacocks let out the most unholy cry, and I was filled with such unease.

Everyone thinks they can see things when they look back. It's nonsense, really, I expect.

2

Forget Dad counting the bedrooms. The Palace had over a hundred rooms if, as well as the lounges and dining rooms and bars and verandahs, you counted hot attics and dark cellars. In less than a week, Dad had the last few stubborn guests shunted off. Then, within hours, some floors were taken up, some ceilings down, and I was living in a strange new world, peopled by men in overalls.

'Natalie, run up to the attics and tell Mr Forrester – he's the one with the beard – that some bloke's on the phone about his wallboard.'

'Oh, no! The new sinks! Natalie, run round to the terrace and ask Ben if a couple of his lads can do a bit of unloading.'

And off he'd stride, to sort out the plasterers, or make arrangements for work to start on yet another floor. Every so often he'd remember me, and the cry would go up.

'Where's Natalie? Anyone seen her?'

If nobody had, then he'd panic.

'Natalie! Can you hear me? Natalie!'

The shouts would echo through cavernous rooms and up lofty stairwells – 'Natalie! *Natalie!*' – till one of the workmen spotted me arranging dusty glasses in rows, like soldiers, on the copper cocktail bar. Or cartwheeling across the empty ballroom. Or leaning over till my panties showed as I peered in cracked urns on the terrace.

'There she blows! Perfectly safe!'

I spent the summer skipping down corridors that had their carpets rolled, and holding endless imaginary conversations with the stone boy in the lily pond. For weeks, the Palace seemed more chaotic each time I picked my way down one of its great swooping staircases. Then, suddenly, the order was reversed. Day by day, dust sheets were whipped off tables and armchairs and sofas. Drills went back into toolchests. And cleaning began, till even my favourite gold cherubs over the mirrors glinted at me one morning, gleaming and bright.

Then, off to cadge a peppermint from one of the painters, I heard Dad taking a call.

'A south-facing double room. Yes, indeed. And dinner on both evenings. Thursday and Friday next.'

I hurled myself at him, barely managing to keep quiet until he'd replaced the receiver.

'Is it opening again? Is that *it*? Are we *going*?'

Wincing, he reached down and lifted me onto the polished brown sea of the reception desk. He looked over his glasses at Mum, who'd been sorting out keys in the corner, and she sighed and gave a tired little nod.

'Natalie,' he said gently. 'I'm afraid we've got something rather awkward to tell you.'

'Stay?' I said, wide-eyed, when I finally understood just what it was they were trying to explain. 'Stay in the Palace for *ever*?'

They started to comfort me! How could they have known so little? How could they have got it so wrong? It had been my one dream all those long, long weeks. To stay! To somersault endlessly down the wide slopes of clover-studded lawn. Wander at will through drawing rooms, writing rooms, boathouses and conservatories. Bounce on the cherry-red sofas. Pick my way like a gymnast, toes pointed, arms outstretched, along the stone ledges of the terraces –

'Natalie?'

I stared at them.

'Natalie, sweet. You don't mind, do you? You won't pine for old friends? You will be all right?'

I nodded at them, dumb with joy.

3

Mum had a hard time with the two of us when Julius was little. Even if my brother did ever finally fall asleep, Mum couldn't hide the fact that she was shattered.

'I'm sorry, Natalie,' she'd say. 'I know I promised. But I feel *sick* with tiredness. Can we do it another day?'

She'd give Dad one of her pleading looks, and, if he had the time, he'd take me off, across the lawns, through the rose garden, and then down the narrow twisty path that led through the dark belt of trees. It almost hurt to step out again, into the brightness of the open field. And that's where we first met Tulip, still as a statue in the sea of corn.

'Is that a scarecrow?'

Dad peered against the sudden glare.

'No. I do believe that it's a little girl.'

'What is she doing out here, all alone?'

Dad shrugged.

'We'll ask.' He took my hand and called across. 'He-llooo! He-llooo!'

She turned to face us, and I could see that she was nursing something.

'Is that a *kitten*?'

I was off in an instant. The Palace had stuffy old cats. But a kitten! Bliss! Dad roared after me. 'Natalie! Think of the crop!' And I came to a halt. Even I realized the farmers were our neighbours, and must be friends. So I stood, burning with impatience, while this stranger my age stepped carefully towards us, spreading the corn with her free hand and picking her way so gently that by the time she reached us I couldn't see a sign of the track she had taken.

The kitten's eyes weren't even open yet.

'What's its name? What are you going to call it?'

Dad touched my shoulder.

'It would be more polite, Natalie, to ask the young lady her name first.'

He looked at her expectantly. But she just tossed her unbrushed hair out of her eyes and stared as if he'd dropped from outer space.

Dad tried again.

'This,' he said, patting me, 'this is Natalie. And I am Mr Barnes, from the hotel.'

Again we waited. And then, finally:

'Tulip,' she said.

I couldn't believe that was her name. I thought she must mean the kitten. And sometimes I wonder if that's the reason I dropped everything to run across and say hello to her a few days later, when she appeared at the edge of the playground. Because, still almost a stranger in my new school, I couldn't miss the chance to say something so silly and bold.

'Hello, Tulip!'

She stared at me, and I faltered. The silence between us grew. And then, too embarrassed to come to my senses, I added the really stupid bit.

'Do you want to be friends?'

I paid for the privilege (if privilege is what it was). Nobody else would have Tulip in their group of friends. They knew from experience that she was out of school more often than in. (That's why I'd not yet seen her.) From that day on, I spent countless hours scuffing alone round the playground, desperately hoping that she'd show up, or that some soft soul in one of the busy swarms of children whooping round me would crack and say the words I longed to hear.

'Forget silly old Tulip. She's never here, anyway. Come and play with us.'

I look back and think I must have been mad. What sort of friendship is it when one of the pair is hardly ever there, and the other is never permitted to go off and find her?

On this, my father was adamant.

'I'm not even discussing it, Natalie. You are not going over to Tulip's house. She can come here as often as she likes. But you're not going there. And that is final.'

Why was he so firm about it? What had he seen that first day that made him so convinced the Pierces' farm was no place for a daughter of his? Most run-down smallholdings are ringed with disembowelled machinery. Most small-time farmers keep frustrated dogs chained up to bark at every passing sparrow. And we didn't meet Tulip's parents. For all Dad knocked and knocked, no one appeared.

A dozen times a week I'd say to him:

'Let's go back and try again. I haven't seen her for days. I probably won't see her again, *ever*, at this rate, if I can't go and find her.'

'No.'

'Maybe she's ill.'

'I doubt it, Natalie.'

'It's not her fault her parents don't think school's important.'

'If I were you, I'd make some other friends. Because nothing's going to change here. You are not going to be allowed to go to Tulip's house. And that is that.'

Was I just being stubborn? What sort of magic did she have for me? All I know is I never made the effort to find another friend. I didn't even put myself out to steal enough good things from the kitchens to wheedle my way into one of the school gangs. Instead, I stayed aloof; and during evenings and weekends I floated round the Palace, presumably content with the glancing interest of bored guests, and my own company, till I'd see her standing on the edge of the lawns.

Then my heart leapt up, and across I'd fly.

'Tulip! Where have you *been*? It's been *ages*. What do you want to *do*?'

We did everything. We went everywhere. We were called in from lawns and potting sheds, shrubberies and terrace gardens. When the cold weather came, they'd look for us in lounges and coffee rooms, alcoves and blanket stores. Sometimes it was awkward to come out because, for the last hour, we'd been wrapped in the folds of the plush ruby curtains, eavesdropping on some unwitting pair of bickering guests. But mostly we'd appear soon after we heard the determined footsteps and the call.

'Time to go home now, Tulip.'

'Can't I stay?'

'Your parents will worry.'

It wasn't true. If Tulip's parents worried, they'd have shown up a dozen times before, when no one had even realized she was still with me till I was ordered off to bed. But Dad would keep a straight face. So would she.

'Can I come back tomorrow?'

'If you like.'

Maybe she would. Maybe she wouldn't. (I'd be waiting, whichever.) Sometimes Dad would notice me drifting round in a trance of solitude, and, realizing how busy he'd been lately, offer to take me fishing. We'd set off in the quiet hour after lunch, and there she'd be, hanging around the field end of the walk through the spinney.

'You can send her home if you like,' I'd say softly, stung that she hadn't bothered to show up for me.

But he'd greet her as cheerfully as usual.

'Coming along?'

She was no good at fishing. (Dad said that everything swam off the minute it saw her shadow.) He'd catch one thing after another, I'd do all right, and she'd get nothing. But she seemed happy enough. And so did he. He never seemed bored on the afternoons Tulip came.

'What was that game you two were playing yesterday, when Mrs Scott-Henderson complained about the noise?'

'*Rats in a Firestorm.*'

'Did you find somewhere more sensible to play it?'

She grinned.

'We moved down to the cellars, and called it *Hogs in a Tunnel,* instead.'

He shook his head.

17

'Very pleasant. Though I suppose it's still less of a bother than that game you were playing all last week.'

'Which? *Fat in the Fire*?'

'It was *Malaria!* most of last week,' I reminded her.

'Why can't you invent some quiet ones?'

'I don't invent them,' I told him. 'Tulip invents the games.'

He turned towards her.

'So,' he said. 'How about it, Tulip?'

She cocked her head to one side. 'There's *Road of Bones*. That's very quiet. And we play *Days of Dumbness* quite a lot. No noise at all in that one.'

He shuddered. '*Days of Dumbness*! *Road of Bones*! Don't the two of you ever play anything pleasant?'

She was grinning again now.

'I suppose you played things like *Happy Families* and *Tickle the Baby* when you were young.'

'Yes,' he said. 'That's the sort of thing we used to play back in the good old days.'

She gave him her flirty look.

'What's the worst thing you ever did, Mr Barnes?'

'When I was a child?'

She nodded.

If I'd asked him that question, he'd never have given a sensible answer. But Tulip could make Dad talk about anything, anything at all, and so he fell quiet, thinking.

'The thing I feel worst about, even after all this time, is dropping my grandfather's tortoise on the garden path,' he told us finally. 'I didn't have the guts to go and tell, so I just shoved it out of sight under the nearest bush.'

He still looked uneasy, remembering.

'How old were you?' I asked.

'Eight.' He made a quick calculation. 'Twenty-seven years ago!'

'Did it smash?' Tulip demanded.

The word she chose repelled him, you could tell. He picked a different one with care.

'Its shell did crack, yes.'

'Was it an accident?'

'Of course it was an accident,' he said sharply. 'You don't suppose I *threw* it?'

'No,' she said hastily.

There was a silence. Then Tulip said:

'You should have put it in the freezer to kill it.'

Dad's face was a picture.

'It's the kindest way, for fish and terrapins,' she assured him. 'Probably for tortoises, as well.'

He'd forgotten his fishing line. He was staring at her now.

'Tulip, how would you ever know that?'

'I suppose I just heard it somewhere. And remembered it.'

Dad turned to me.

'Did you know?'

I wanted so much to say I did. But Tulip would have known I was fibbing.

'No,' I said sullenly.

He turned back to her.

'And do the things you hear worry you?'

'No,' she said. 'Sometimes I think about them for a bit. But mostly I'm interested more than I'm worried.'

There was a flurry underneath her float.

'Is that a bite?' he asked, happy to be distracted. 'Have you been lucky for once? Is that a bite?'

'No,' she said, not even looking. 'No, it's not.'

6

I did go to her house, of course. But only once. I can't remember what fired me up. Had I, for once, something to tell her that I should be brave enough to sidle to the edge of the lawn, then so casually slip out of sight in the shadows? Those huge, overhanging trees must have given a sense of foreboding to the venture. But I didn't falter, and, out in the sunlight again, stayed on the far side of the fence till I was beyond the view from the highest Palace window. Hotels are filled with bored people. You can always be sure that, whatever you are doing, there will always be somebody standing and watching.

I hated Tulip's house. It wasn't just that the carpets were stained and the furniture battered. It was that Tulip herself seemed different, just a shell, as if she had slipped away invisibly and left some strange, strained imitation in her place to say to me, 'What shall we do now?' or, 'Want another biscuit?'

I pushed the packet of damp crumbs aside. I'd have suggested going into her bedroom, but the glimpse of a stained sheet spread over a chair to dry as she kicked closed the door had warned me that wouldn't be welcome.

'Shall we go in the yard?'

I wanted to get out of the kitchen. Tulip's mother was giving me the creeps with her beg-pardon smile and her tireless, tuneless humming; as if, in that horrible, smelly, sunless back room, she'd completely forgotten a song was supposed to have a melody, let alone a beginning and ending. Hearing that awful, interminable drone was like listening to a robot pretend to be a person.

The back yard had clumps of weeds waist high. But there were far too many smashed bottles lying about for us to play most of our creeping games. So, in desperation, I said:

'Let's go and find your kitten.'

She looked at me blankly.

'Well,' I corrected myself, feeling stupid. 'Cat, by now.'

'We don't have a cat.'

'You were carrying one the day I met you.'

Her eyes went pebble hard.

'I expect I had to give it away.'

I knew she was lying. So, in my eyes, of course, it was a merciless cat killer I met when, retreating from the unpromising yard, we came face to face with Mr Pierce, striding in through another door. I watched as he filled a cracked cup with water, drank it down, refilled it, drank more, then turned back from the sink. His eyes came to rest on me, and never moved till I snatched up my jacket and, burbling excuses, rushed away.

'I'm sorry I had to go like that,' I said to her next morning at school. 'I suddenly remembered I was supposed to –'

And off I went again. Burble-burble. Burble-burble. Tulip looked cross and bored until I stopped. Then she said:

'Dad's all right when you're used to him.'

But I had no intention of giving him even one more try. From that day on, I stopped nagging Dad about letting me go there, and used the excuse he had taught me to save Tulip's feelings,

'They won't let me near dogs like Elsa.'

And stayed away.

7

And I saw lots of her at school. She had no other friends. Nobody else could stand the embarrassment of pretending that they believed her awful lies.

'The army's borrowing one of our fields today. When I get home, they're going to let me drive a tank.'

'Oh, I really believe that, Tulip!'

'So likely!'

They'd walk off, scoffing. I'd stare at the ground, and, guess what, I'd feel *sorry* for her. I knew she was making a fool of me in front of everyone. (Only an idiot would make a show of believing her rubbish.) But instead of just walking away, exasperated, like everyone else, I'd try taking her arm and distracting her.

'Want to play *Road of Bones* on the way home?'

She'd shake me off, rude and ungrateful. Even back then I had to ask myself why I stayed around. It wasn't out of pity, I knew that. Nobody *has* to carry on telling ridiculous lies, even after it's obvious that no one believes them.

'I've won a big competition. I found a scratchcard in my cornflakes and I was lucky. So now I've won this beautiful yellow silk dress.'

Next time we bought sweets in Harry's supermarket, I'd linger by the breakfast cereal shelves.

'There's nothing about a competition on any of these packets.'

'No. It was a scratchcard inside.'

'Strange that no one else got one.'

'They only sent out a few as a special anniversary thing. That's why the prize is a yellow silk dress. It's the very same one that the model wore in their first advert.'

That's what Dad came to call the Tulip touch – that tiny detail that almost made you wonder if she might, just for once, be telling the truth.

'And then this man went grey and keeled over. And as I was phoning for the ambulance, his fingers kept twitching, and his wedding ring made a tiny little pinging noise against the metal of the drain.'

'So I wasn't at school because the police needed one extra person my age and size, for a line-up. They wouldn't say why they'd arrested the girl, but one of them did tell me that he thought she was Polish.'

'Ah!' Dad would murmur in unfeigned admiration. 'Polish? The perfect Tulip touch!'

She'd give him a pained wooden stare. 'Sorry?'

'Nothing.'

He'd turn away, of course, to hide his grin. But I'd be left to see the look of venom on her face. Tulip loathed being teased. It was as if the moment these stupid stories were out of her mouth, she believed them completely, and anyone who queried even a tiny part of them was going to be her enemy, and hated for ever.

So it was Dad, not me, who risked a bit of mischief a couple of weeks later.

'So where's the great yellow dress, Tulip? How come you haven't brought it round to show us yet?'

She looked surprised. 'Didn't I tell you? I had it ready in a bag. Then Mum knocked over a bottle of bleach, and some got on the sleeve. So she's posted it off to a big firm in Chichester that does a lot of mending for the royal family, to see if they can patch it from the hem.'

Dad watched her, spellbound. Once she was gone, he turned to Mum.

'Poor little imp. What sort of squashing must she get at home, to think she has to make up all this stuff to impress us?'

Mum just said irritably:

'You'd think she had more than enough brains to know better!'

And you would, too. She was miles cleverer than me. If it weren't for her missed days, and undone homework, she would have beaten me in every test. But, even in good weeks, Miss Henson had problems with Tulip.

'Please try and settle down. You're distracting everybody round you.'

'Now that's not what I told you to do, is it?'

'Tulip! I warn you, I have had *enough*!'

If she'd spoken to me that sharply, I'd have died of fright. But Tulip didn't care. A moment later, she'd be rushing out of her seat across the room.

'I can see Julia's rubber on the floor!'

And a minute or so later:

'Now I'm going across to help Jennifer with her project.'

There was a plaintive and immediate wail.

'Stop her, Miss Henson! I don't want her help!'

Out came the tongue. (Tulip's, not Jennifer's.)

'Tulip! Back to your table! Sit down! And stop being such a nuisance!'

I sat so quiet I was hardly there. That's why she left us side by side, I expect. So I could water Tulip's fidgets down. But somehow we went together well, and things worked out. We were the triangles in primary band. We shared counting the lunch money two months in a row (though, now I look back, I realize that was probably Miss Henson's way of getting the job done properly through Tulip's month of office). And we were the Ugly Sisters in the Christmas play.

At first, I could tell, both Miss Henson and Mr Barraclough were deeply dubious about giving Tulip the part she begged for so piteously.

'I have to warn you, Tulip. If you miss more than a couple of rehearsals, we'll have to take the part off you. So are you sure?'

She nodded vigorously.

'And I must have a note from your father saying he won't mind you coming in for the evening performances.'

Tulip's keen look turned sour.

'Nobody else has to bring in any note.'

Miss Henson sighed.

'I'm sorry, Tulip. It's just that Mr Barraclough hasn't forgotten yet.'

When she'd walked off, I asked Tulip:

'Hasn't forgotten what?'

'Last time. Before you came. I was a Dancing Bean.'

'Was it difficult?'

(It seemed the best way of asking, 'What went wrong?')

'I did it fine,' she said. 'I learned the song. I knew the dance. But then something came up. So I couldn't do it.'

I'd been fobbed off with that 'something came up' too often myself. But in the first flush of being her Ugly Sister, I felt generous.

'You'd think he'd *want* you to have a good part this time.'

She executed what I could only take to be a short snatch of Bean Dance.

'It wouldn't have mattered so much, except for the others.'

'Others?'

'The other beans. The dance was a bit complicated, you see. So they couldn't do it without me.'

'Oh.'

I had a sudden vision of everyone trying to get through the big night with only one Ugly Sister. Me. But, in the end, there wasn't any trouble. Her mother sent in the note. Tulip showed up every day that we had a rehearsal. And she and I turned out to be the stars of the show. Tulip's witchy foot-stamping frenzies and my vacuous no-one-at-home stare were far more fun to watch than prissy Cinderella's tears. Each time we stumbled off stage, Mr Barraclough was waiting with the grease stick. My first few discreet spots grew, scene by scene, into a riot of measles. He'd spray more cobwebs onto Tulip's frizzy green wig, and push us both on again, hissing,

29

'Brilliant, the pair of you! Keep it up!'

And so we did, three evenings in a row, getting the loudest laughter all the way through, and the longest applause at the end. After the last show I was so forlorn I refused to let anyone take off my make-up. The giant spots rubbed off on my pillow-case, and Tulip had to hand in her green wig in the morning. But no one could wipe the performance out of us.

'Will you two stop lolling against one another! If you don't, I shall separate you.'

'Natalie, don't nudge Tulip when you know the answer yourself. You're not a dummy. Put up your own hand, please.'

'Tulip, she's not a puppet on a string. Just because you need to go, it doesn't follow that Natalie has to go with you.'

Halfway through January, Miss Henson finally moved us apart. We wailed and fussed.

'It isn't fair! We weren't being naughty. We were just being *sisters*, like in the play.'

'Hard cheese,' she said brutally. 'I'm afraid that was *last* year.'

And that, of course, set off the next game. *That Was Last Year*. The silliest remark would set it off.

'Marcie can't find her gloves.'

'No. That was last year. She's looking for her panties now.'

'Have you seen Miss Henson's new car?'

'That was last year. She came on a broomstick this morning.'

They were so stupid and unfunny, we only whispered them. But still they sent us into such spasms of amusement that the others would gather round us in the playground.

'What's the big joke?'

'Nothing.'

We'd stick our knuckles in our mouths and snigger some more.

'Oh, leave them. They're just being silly.'

And so we were. So silly that, before I realized what was happening, the taint of unpopularity had thickened and spread.

'Oh, *please* don't make me sit by Natalie. She just giggles all the time, and makes faces with Tulip.'

'I'm not sitting with her, either!'

Miss Henson caught the flu. Her father had to go to hospital. And everyone she tried to seat us beside put up a really hard fight. It's strange to think that we go down whole different paths because of accidents in other people's lives. My friendship with Tulip could have been derailed, or, at the very least, diluted a little.

But flu. A broken hip. A bit of squawking round the class.

And she gave up.

'All right, then. If you promise to behave yourselves, I'll give you one more chance. Just one.'

8

What were we like then, the pair of us, Tulip and Natalie? I lift a photograph out of the box, and see us laughing. We look happy enough. But do old photos tell the truth? 'Smile!' someone orders you. 'I'm not wasting time taking photos of sour faces.' And so you smile. But what's behind? You take the one Dad snapped by accident when Tulip came down the cellar steps just as he was fiddling in the dark with his camera. Suddenly the flash went off, and he caught her perfectly (if you don't count the rabbity pink eyes). She's a shadow in the arched entrance of that dark tunnel. And how does she look in that, the only one to be taken when no one was watching?

Wary, would you say? Or something even stronger? One look at that pale and apprehensive face, and you might even think *haunted*. But there's something else that springs to mind. I turn the photo in my hand, and try to push the word away. But it comes back at me, time and again. I can't get rid of it. If you didn't know her better, you'd have said she looked *desolate*.

And yet Tulip loved the Palace. Every inch of it. I'd watch her endlessly running her fingertips along the swirling banisters and gritty stone ledges and dimpled bar tops as if, by sheer touching, she could make the whole place hers.

'Natalie, you're so *lucky*.'

I'd shrug. I knew it, but it seemed rude to agree; as if, in admitting it, I'd be halfway to saying that I would have gladly died a thousand deaths rather than swap my life with hers. And these days Tulip rarely hung around the cornfields. She came as often as she could, sucking up to Mum, flirting with Dad.

'Good morning, Mr Barnes.'

'Morning, Tulip, my flower. But I do have to warn you that no one gets late breakfast in this hotel, even here in the kitchens, without first settling with the Manager.'

'What's the price today?'

'Let me see . . . It's Saturday, isn't it? And High Season. So I'm afraid it's going to be – a hug and three kisses.'

He'd take off his glasses and she'd count the kisses out onto his cheek.

'One. Two. Three. And the hug. There!'

'Right,' he'd say. 'Now that you've paid, you must have another sausage.'

34

He'd flip it on her plate, his party trick. But she'd be watching, not the arc it was making through the air, but the sausage itself. For Tulip loved the food. I was forever losing sight of her for a few minutes, only to find her in the kitchens, her mouth stuffed with something she'd already begged, staring at treats to come: the creamy trifles and the chocolate roulades; the cherry meringue pies she loved above all else.

'Want to come up to the toy room?'

'In a bit.'

A few minutes later, she'd trail up the last of the steep wooden stairs and join me, rooting through drifts of abandoned games and toys. The sort of people who bring children to the Palace have never been the types to go scouring the grounds on their last day for lost rounders bats and mislaid dolls. So if we were bored with hurling hard apples at the stone boy in the lily pond, or racing up and down the gravel paths, then we'd go up and find something different in the toy room. We had a craze on the pogo stick, and learned to fly the battered kites. Tulip mastered the fretwork saw, and we even had short passions for the faded old sewing cards and the prissy little flower press.

'What do you think? Dress-ups?'

The trunks were brilliant, spilling with feather boas, and muffs, and tunics with military frogging.

'Do you suppose the people who owned all these really old things are *dead*?'

I held my favourite taffeta frock against me.

'They must be. Most things get sent on now. Dad says he spends most of Tuesday posting packages to careless people.'

She jammed a brown felt hat down hard on my head.

'Now you're Miss Henson's mother.'

I threw a velvet cape around her shoulders and handed her a tattered parasol.

'And you're Mr Barraclough's great-aunt.'

We minced round the attics in our ill-fitting high heels.

'Did you see my nephew's splendid recent production of *Cinderella*?'

'Indeed I did.'

'And did you notice those two astonishingly talented young actresses, Tulip and Natalie? I thought that Tulip was by far the best.'

'I preferred Natalie.'

'No. Tulip.'

'Natalie.'

'Tulip.'

We fell, wrestling, onto the heaps of old clothes. My nose filled with the stink of mothballs.

'Even-stevens?' I panted.

36

She let go of me.

'Even-stevens.'

The hours spun past. Time had two speeds for me. The racing kaleidoscopic tumble of days spent with Tulip, when the first of the peacocks' bloodcurdling evening shrieks made me look at my watch with astonishment. And then the endless drag of days alone, when only a few miserable minutes crawled by between each desperate inspection of the clock.

There was scant sympathy at hand.

'If you're bored, play with Julius.'

'I'm not bored.'

I was, though. Not bored enough to play with my brother, but bored enough to feel that every minute spent away from Tulip was not real living, just a waiting time.

'Well, play with Julius anyway.'

And so I did. Sometimes with good grace, sometimes with bad. But always feeling there was something missing, and that the real day I should be having was taking place somewhere half a dozen fields away, beyond the spinney.

With Tulip.

9

She bought Julius a plastic toad for his birthday. We stood in front of it in the charity shop.

'It's a bit scratched,' she worried.

'He won't mind that. He probably won't even notice.'

'You don't think he'd prefer something furry?'

'No. I think he'll like this.'

Like it? He fell in love. He instantly named it Mr Haroun (after a recent guest who'd spoiled him rotten) and carried it round all day. At bathtime it disappeared under a towel, and when one of the Austrian ladies staying a week had to wait twenty minutes for a drink because half the hotel staff were searching for the toad, she persuaded her sister to lay aside the rose tapestry she was working on, and run up a sort of baby backpack that kept Mr Haroun safe, but left Julius's hands free. Julius's loyalties were fierce. The Austrian guests moved on (though not before appliquéing Mr Haroun's name in glossy silk letters on the tie-down flap). And Tulip reaped all the credit. Everyone who passed through the Palace admired the way the backpack was designed to keep the toad safe, but let him see and breathe. And, if we were around, Julius inevitably pointed to Tulip and said proudly:

'She gave it me.'

Guests would fall over themselves to congratulate Tulip. They admired everything about the backpack: its design, the silk lettering, the beautiful stitching. Tulip soaked up the praise, grinning modestly and flapping her hands in an embarrassed fashion. It never bothered Julius that Tulip was accepting compliments for someone else's work. Why should it? To him, only his precious toad mattered, and Tulip had definitely given him that. But what is strange is that it never bothered me. Guests would lean forward on sofas to flatter Tulip, and their companions would turn aside and tap me on the arm.

'Now, *isn't* your friend clever?'

And so in thrall to Tulip that everything she did was fine by me, I'd feel as proud of her as if she could sew.

IO

One of my jobs was taking Julius to nursery on my way to school. Down the drive, over the bridge (walking on the side with the *pavement*) and up the path to the porch, where all the others were struggling to get out of their brightly coloured wellies and raincoats.

For a goodbye, Julius would lift his face and purse his lips to give me a giant smacker.

'Kissypots!'

He'd turned from a sleepless monster into an easy and affectionate child. 'Devil to angel' said my parents. And even I enjoyed his constant stream of bright prattle as we strolled along together, hand in hand. I'd been forbidden to make arrangements to meet Tulip on school mornings because I'd been late so often on days when she didn't show. But, as often as not, out she'd jump from behind someone's front wall, or one of the pillars of the bridge, startling me every time.

She'd fall in step.

'Want to play *Stinking Mackerel*?'

'All the way? Even the people at the bus stop?'

'All the way. Everyone. Even Mrs Bodell.'

So everyone who passed got enough of the game to unnerve them. We weren't *rude,* exactly. It was all done with a wrinkle of the nose, a tiny sniff, maybe even a fleeting look of disgust. Some days, with everyone bent double against the wind, it didn't work. On others, we must have left a trail of worried people. Often we'd turn and catch them plucking at their clothes, trying to look as if they were simply pulling a jacket straight, or tightening a belt, when we knew they were anxiously checking for odours.

Mrs Bodell, though, rumbled us thoroughly. She took no cheek, and some of her threats were awesome.

'I'm catching the bus into Urlingham now. But as soon as I get back I shall speak to your head teacher. Don't think I don't know your parents, Natalie Barnes. *And* how ashamed they'll be to hear of your behaviour.'

So we'd do Mrs Bodell. But only half-heartedly, safe behind her giant rump. And even then I'd cheat, unwrapping my lunch bag as I walked by the stop, and lowering my nose to it as though to imply that all the sniffing and nose-wrinkling was nothing to do with her, but because of my sandwich.

Safe in the playground, I'd start to moan at Tulip.

'You're ruder than I am. How come it's always *my* name she broadcasts to the world?'

But I knew the answer, anyway. Mum wasn't the first to point out that games with Tulip had a habit of starting well for two, and ending badly for one. I was the usual victim. But once or twice she tried her luck with Julius. I called a halt to *Putting on the Bag*. But then she started something called *Babe in the Wood*. One after another, while we were walking him, we'd vanish into the trees. Soon he'd be fretting. Then I'd materialize as calmly as if I'd never been gone. He'd spin round, and there was Tulip, back without a word. Somehow she'd distract him, and I'd be gone again. He'd turn, upset and confused, to find that Tulip had disappeared as well. The game used to drive him wild with fear and rage. And why are my memories of it so strong, unless we played it for weeks? Maybe we only stopped because Mum caught us at it. She heard the screams and, running up, found Julius with tears spurting from his eyes, spitting a blaze of gibberish.

'Out here, right now! Both of you!'

I stepped out at once. But this time Tulip had vanished for good and proper. That didn't bother Mum. She raised her voice and warned her anyway.

'You listen to me, Tulip Pierce! If I ever catch you tormenting Julius again, you'll be in trouble! And, as for you, Natalie!'

As for me, I was sent upstairs earlier than Julius for a whole week. Whichever of them it was, Mum or Dad, deliberately called out 'Bedtime, now, Natalie!' in front of the guests, who looked up in astonishment from their first gins and tonics. You could almost hear them whispering to one another: 'Bedtime? Surely the child must be ten years old, at least!' From that day on, I wouldn't join in games with Julius unless he quite enjoyed them. But Tulip didn't mind because, what with Christmas coming up, she was happy to be on her very best behaviour. Tulip *loved* Christmas at the Palace. At her house, we knew, the decorations amounted to little more than a set of chipped Nativity figures and some wobbly-headed Santa she never properly described. The wrappings for her presents were ironed over from last year. And the only special foods were the turkey and Christmas pudding.

Still, Tulip's pleading made my parents uneasy at first.

'Can I come early? For breakfast?'

'But, Tulip, won't your parents mind? Won't they want you at home with them?'

Tulip put on her false face.

'Oh, no. They don't mind. They say it's just a shame I don't have any brothers or sisters to share the day, and if I want to be with Natalie, they're happy for me.'

It didn't sound all that likely. But Mum allowed herself to be convinced.

'In that case, I'm sure we'd be delighted to have you.'

I look back now, and wonder what price Tulip paid for Christmas at the Palace. More than the other guests, I'll bet. I knew that even back then. For once, as we were strolling home together after school, I heard a vicious bellow, and looked up to see Mr Pierce leaning out of his truck window.

'Better get home before me, Tulip, or I'll snatch you bald-headed!'

I stood, rigid. Snatch her *bald-headed*? But Tulip had already fled. I followed her as far as the corner, picking up things that spilled out of her school bag, and thinking about the odd things I'd heard her saying in our games. 'I'll peel you alive, like a banana!' 'Smile at me wrong today, and I'll crush you!' 'I'll make your eyes look like slits in a grapefruit!' I'd always put them down to Tulip being clever – good with words. But was I wrong? Was it Tulip I'd been hearing, or her terrifying father?

No Christmas on earth would have been worth it for me. But I'd been spoiled. As long as I could remember, every December had blazed scarlet and gold. Bright coloured lanterns winked along the terraces. There were at least five decorated trees. Everything glittered and sparkled, and the food was amazing.

'Can we have pies with battlements?'

'Natalie, when did we ever *not* have pies with battlements at Christmas?'

'And will there be some of those great long pink fishes on a dish?'

'Salmon, Tulip. Yes, there'll be salmon.'

'And wine jellies, like last year?'

'Yes. Wine jellies.'

'And can I turn on the blinking lights?'

Dad grinned.

'Yes, Tulip. You can turn on the blinking lights.'

We all indulged her at Christmas. It was, my father said wryly, the only time Tulip ever acted her age. Her eyes kept widening. Her mouth kept falling open. And once, like Julius, she was even found scrabbling under the tree, shaking all the empty wrapped boxes, just to be sure that what she'd been told was true, and they were really only there for show.

Each year, Mum found some way to smarten her up a bit.

'Here, Tulip. This dress belongs to Mrs Stoddart's Cecily. But she's wearing her green one, and we think this will fit you. It's just for today, mind. You mustn't run off with it.'

There was a sticky moment, but Dad managed to save it.

'And Mrs Stoddart mustn't run off with you!'

So Tulip pretended that she hadn't heard, or didn't mind, and let herself slip into enchantment. She cuddled the frock till Mum pushed her into the office. There, Tulip raised her arms and Mum lifted off her thin, mock-crochet top, and unhooked her cheap skirt. The deep blue velvet of the frock tumbled all over her, falling in folds that turned her spindly thinness into height, and hid her battered shoes.

'And can I wear it all day?'

'All day.'

And all day we caught her stroking invisible puckers and creases out of the velvet, and seeking out mirrors. Time and again she'd think of clever ways of getting rid of me for a few minutes. And when I rushed back, she'd be smiling at herself in the glass as she watched the reflection of her solitary make-believe dance swirls and curtsies.

Dad kept creeping up on her from the sides.

'Unbutton your beak, Tulip.'

Her eyes closed. A blissful look stole over her face as she opened her mouth as wide as a young thrush.

He popped in the canapé, or vol-au-vent, or whatever. She learned the hard way about spoiling her appetite for lunch. And when, after dinner, it was clear she'd given no thought at all to getting home, Dad pulled her aside for a moment.

'Tulip, aren't you going to get into hot water if you're late?'

On went the false face.

'They know I'm probably going to stay the night. They said I could.'

His troubled eyes met hers. He looked down first.

'All right, then. If you're *sure*.'

And he took Tulip by one hand and me by the other and, with Julius leading the way on his brand new tricycle (indoors for one day only, all guests warned), he marched us towards the piano. I expect we were dreadful at singing. But they would have drowned us out, that strange and hearty assortment of people who choose to spend Christmas in a big hotel. Some patted our shoulders and pointed to the place on the carol sheet. And others, who had no idea how much we'd already eaten, slipped unwrapped sweets into our hands. I remember the blue-rinsed ladies had gold teeth that winked in the candlelight. And the men often stank of tobacco. Mr Hearns' hands swept effortlessly up and down the keys. And if you looked sideways at Tulip in her beautiful blue dress, chirruping out *Good King Wenceslas* and *Silent Night*, her face radiant, you would never have thought that she'd have to go home, and face a very different, more ugly, sort of music in the morning.

II

Not that she couldn't hand it out herself. Dad said it first.

'I reckon some mean thoughts go on behind those pretty smiles of hers.'

And he was right. On our first day back at school after the holidays, Tulip was waiting for me at the gate.

'You've got it, haven't you? You didn't forget?'

I handed it over. Her eyes sparkled, and she went dancing off in search of Jamie Whitton. She thrust the little box into his hand.

'What's this?'

'What does it look like? It's a Christmas present.'

He shook it suspiciously. 'It's a bit late for that.'

If she'd said anything, he would have been even more wary. But she just shrugged. She had a gift for making people believe her.

He glanced round. Miss Henson was standing on the steps. The bell would go any minute.

'Why did you get me a present?'

'I just did.'

'I didn't get you one.'

'That's all right.'

She managed to look both shy and careless at the same time. I knew then it was going to work.

'Tulip –'

'Shh!' she said to me sharply. And then, to Jamie: 'Go on, then. Open it. It won't bite you.'

I could have said, 'No, don't. It's not a real present. Just something stupid we did yesterday.' Then Jamie would have stuffed it back at her, and she'd have dropped it. And then, of course, she would have walked away. From him. From me.

So I stood and watched as he tugged gingerly at the knotted silver thread, and unwrapped the glistening paper. He tipped the lid back. The little black curls of dried dog mess sat in their crumpled tissue nest.

'Happy Christmas!' crowed Tulip.

'Happy Christmas!' I echoed.

Bravely, he tried to defend himself. 'It isn't Christmas any more. And so the joke's on you.'

And probably just about anyone else in the class could have carried it off. But not Jamie. Tulip knew how to choose her victims. From the moment she'd spotted the little desiccated pile beside the radiator, and sent me off in search of a flat-bladed knife, she'd had Jamie Whitton in mind. And she was right. He kept his end up gamely all day long. 'I never even touched it.' 'I guessed what was in it, anyway.' 'You two are just stupid.' But after the last bell rang, Tulip hurried me across the playground and behind the wall.

'Keep your head down.'

'Why?'

'Just *wait*!' she said fiercely.

Obediently, I waited. Cars pulled up outside the school. Doors slammed. Cars drove away.

'Now!' she said. 'Take a look!'

She'd timed it perfectly. Just as we raised our heads, Jamie's mother slid the car into gear and pulled out from the kerb. And though, when he spotted us watching, he turned his head away as fast as possible, I still had time to see, through the freshly washed windscreen, the first few fat tears of misery roll down his cheek.

And, when I turned to look at her, Tulip's smile.

And there's another time I shan't forget, when I cut my knee, wading over to the stone boy in the lily pond. I was carrying a hat we had spent hours dressing with feathers, so I didn't dare use my hands to save myself when I stumbled and fell against the sharp side of his pedestal.

Blood poured from the gash. I looked down and felt quite frightened. With each step I took against the water, blood washed away, then welled again.

'Hurry!' yelled Tulip. 'Walk faster! Run!'

No one can run through water. By the time I got back to the edge, my heart was thumping. Tulip prised the hat from my hands. It wasn't even splashed.

'Good heavens, child!'

One of the guests had strolled over to see what was happening. Scattering peacocks, she hurried me up the terrace and propped me against a ledge. First came a linen cloth from one of the bars. I soaked that scarlet in seconds. Then came the towels. And then my parents arrived.

Tulip danced round, getting in everyone's way as Dad went to fetch a car as close as he could without flattening the flower beds, and everyone else spilled out advice.

'You realize she'll need at least half a dozen stitches.'

'I shouldn't bother with the surgery. I'd take her straight to the hospital.'

'Don't worry, Mrs Barnes. These things so often look a whole lot worse than they are.'

Dad appeared round the corner. Behind him, a car engine throbbed. I was handed down over the terrace, and Mum ran to keep up as Dad strode with me in his arms

51

towards the back seat. He tipped me in, and Mum threw herself in beside me and slammed the door after her.

Someone opened the door again, to push in more towels.

'Oh, thank you!' said Mum. 'Thank you!'

I heard a sharp tap, and looked through the other window. Tulip was just outside, prancing about like a monkey. She made a stupid face, splaying her hands, tipping her head sideways and sticking out her tongue.

Turning away, I caught the look my mother gave her in return. I shut my eyes then. I can shut them now. But I can still see both their faces.

Tulip's? Well, ugly and uncaring, certainly.

But Mum's?

Far, far more disturbing, somehow. I can't really explain. All I can tell you is that Mum was looking at Tulip the way no one normally looks at a child.

But Tulip was always doing stupid things. Soon she was spending as much time sitting outside Miss Golightly's office as she spent back in class. And one day, chatting to Dad while he was doing the monthly cellar check, I very carelessly let this slip.

Dad casually changed the subject. But I knew what I'd said struck home. For two days, nothing happened. But then Will Stannard came back into class from the dentist to report that my dad's car was parked right outside the school.

Next morning, Mr Barraclough walked in and said, 'I think we'll sit you next to Barney, Natalie.'

Tulip was outraged.

'Why does she have to move?'

Mr Barraclough bit back a sharp response, and said instead:

'We all just think that everyone might benefit from a little change.'

Furious, Tulip swept everything off her desk onto the floor.

'If Natalie can't sit by me, then I'm not doing any more work!'

If any of the rest of us had done that, we would have been in such deep trouble. But it was as if the staff were half-scared, half-despairing of Tulip. So Mr Barraclough let her be. She sat, stone-faced, arms folded, through the lesson, and he ignored her. When the bell rang, he sent her to the office as usual. And I spent yet another lonely break. None of the other children would come near me. Tulip's sheer recklessness made them nervous, too. And if there was even the slightest possibility that she might be sent back out in time to join us, they'd always take the precaution of staying clear.

In class time, to be fair, the teachers tried over and over to give me opportunities to make new friends.

'Natalie, why don't you pair up with Susan to put up the new corridor display?'

'Marcie and Natalie, I'll leave you here to set out all the chairs.'

I'd chat to them, and they'd chat back. I'd even wonder what it would be like to have them as friends. But when we came back in the classroom I couldn't help but glance across. And there was Tulip, seeking me out with her hard, hungry little eyes, as if she could actually *see* if I'd stayed faithful, if I still belonged to her. Back then, of course, I never thought to wonder what it was Tulip saw in me. But now I think, could some small part of it have been that, if she could keep someone as faceless and nondescript as me as her friend, then it really couldn't prove so much that everyone else hated her?

And hate her they did. Because she spoiled *everything*.

'I'm afraid we can't start until Tulip's quite ready.'

'If there's any more messing about, then we won't have the ropes out – *Tulip*!'

'I'm sorry if it's a disappointment to most of you, but after a certain person's behaviour on the last field trip . . .'

The staff lost patience with her.

'Why do you make things so difficult for yourself?'

She'd scowl, but not answer, making that old game of ours, *Days of Dumbness*, into a regular thing.

'I'm still waiting . . .'

Still no response. People from other classes would walk past in the corridor and eye her curiously.

'You do realize, don't you, Tulip, that this is just one more silly way of trying to grab everyone's attention. But there are a lot of people in this school. Not just you.'

Another few minutes of silence, and then whichever teacher it was would usually crack.

'Well, you'd better go out for break now. And when you come in again, I expect you to be more sensible. Off you go.'

Out in the playground, she'd run wild, swearing and shrieking, and cheeking the dinner ladies, while I stood by, passively watching.

One day a message came, bellowed out from the steps, and picked up excitedly by everyone round me.

'Natalie! Miss Golightly wants you in her room. Right now!'

'Miss Golightly wants Natalie!'

'Natalie, you've got to go to the office.'

'Not just to the office. Miss Golightly wants to see her!'

'Hurry, Natalie!'

The world drained of colour. I was terrified. I stumbled on the steps, and got lost round corners I knew as well as my own face. With the secretary watching, I tapped on the panels of Miss Golightly's door.

'Is that Natalie Barnes?'

Timidly, I pushed. But already Miss Golightly was striding towards me. Thrusting the door wide, she flattened her hand on my back and propelled me across to the window.

'Is that your friend?' she cried, pointing. 'Is it? *Is* it?'

Tulip was running up to gangs of little ones, and stamping at their games.

'Look at her! Spoiling things for everybody! Rampaging about!'

She made a visible effort to calm herself.

'Sit down, Natalie. It's time that you and I had a little talk.'

I don't remember much of it. Only how very frightened I was suddenly to be put in a chair that had cushions, and talked to as if I were grown up. It seemed to break all the rules, and left me too rattled even to listen properly, let alone speak up with sensible answers. Only when Miss Golightly moved on from what she kept calling 'Tulip's real difficulties' and her 'influence on the people around her' did I stop feeling like a panicked rabbit. By then, she must have been hinting at my parents' concerns, because the first words I remember saying were:

'They can't mind Tulip that much, because they let her come.'

She looked astonished.

'What? To the Palace? Really?'

'Yes,' I said resolutely. 'She comes a lot. Dad's very nice to her.'

This irritated Miss Golightly, you could tell. Clearly Dad must have given her a very different picture.

Frowning, she said, 'Perhaps they prefer to keep an eye on the two of you together. Have you thought of that?'

Dutifully, I tried to look as if she might be right. But I knew better. I'd worked out long ago that Mum let Tulip keep coming because she couldn't stand watching me mope round the Palace without her. It just got on her nerves to see me floating aimlessly through room after room. And Dad had a soft spot for Tulip. He knew her faults. And he may even have thought she was as bad for me outside school as she was in. But I'd seen the look on his face the day we drove round a corner to find Mr Pierce thrashing his dog in the shadow of a hedgerow. And I saw the extra gentleness and courtesy with which he always greeted Tulip's mother when she tried creeping past us in the street. Dad didn't say much. But I knew exactly what he thought of Tulip's home life.

And tell her she couldn't come? Well, he just couldn't do it.

Perhaps Miss Golightly thought he'd not been straight with her, with his complaints. In any case, my ticking off was over. She rose to her feet.

'Natalie, I hope you'll think seriously about all the things I've been saying.' This time the hand on my shoulder was almost gentle as she walked me to the door. 'Because, I warn you, you'll come to no good at all as Tulip's hold-your-coat merchant. Think about that.'

★

Tulip was lying in wait in the playground.

'What did she want?'

My heart was back to thumping.

'Nothing much, honestly.'

Tulip was irritated.

'Well, then, Birdbrain, what did she *say*?'

Perhaps I was peeved with her for getting me into such trouble. Anyhow, just for once I managed to speak up for myself.

'I don't think that birdbrains are bright enough to remember what's been said to them.'

Furious, she lashed out at the nearest thing, which was a folding sign about the next parents' evening. One of the dinner ladies bore down on her threateningly, and I vanished round the corner. I wandered nervously round the edges of the infants' playing area. But by the time Tulip ambled back in sight, accompanied by Marcie, she was all smiles. I wondered if she'd forgotten I'd been somewhere of interest, though I had more sense than to resurrect the subject. But that night, when Mum sent me along to give George the barman a message, I sidled up to one of the guests I knew best on my way out, and asked him,

'Mr Scott Henderson, what's a hold-your-coat merchant?'

Winking at George, he said to me, 'Now don't you tell me that you and your little friend are getting into fights!'

I felt myself go scarlet.

'Fights?'

'That's what it means,' he explained. 'A hold-your-coat merchant is a person who likes to watch someone else get into trouble.' He made his voice sound like a little boy's. ' "Go on!" ' he squeaked. ' "You fight him! He deserves it! I'll stand here safely and I'll hold your coat." '

He took a sip of whisky.

'Why are you asking, anyway?'

I'm not allowed to linger in the bars, and just as I began to scour my brain for some likely story, George raised his eyebrows at me over the beer glass he was polishing.

I danced away.

'No reason,' I carolled behind me. 'It just came up at school.'

Next morning, I learned the reasons for Tulip's smiles. I kept my eyes peeled for her all the way from the nursery. But when I reached the school gates, she was already in the playground, locked arm in arm with Marcie.

She greeted me coolly.

'Marcie's with us today. That's all right, isn't it?'

I nodded. Marcie's quarrels with Claire, though frequent and explosive, were famously short-lived. I thought that I'd have Tulip back by break. But Marcie stayed with us all day. I was upset. (Tulip kept calling me Birdbrain.) But still

I tagged along, pretending I hardly noticed and didn't care, till we drifted past Harry's Supermarket after school.

'Coming in?'

You could tell from her eyes it was a challenge.

'No,' I said. 'Not today.'

'Why not?'

'He watches us. I can feel it. He doesn't like us in there.'

'That's *his* problem.'

'But it makes me not want to go in there.'

'Baby!'

But Marcie was tugging on her arm, so she gave up and we went round the back. We started balancing along the low walls dividing the sections of the car park. Right in the middle of a wobbly arabesque, Tulip suddenly announced to Marcie that the manager of Harry's had that very morning offered her a Saturday job.

'Don't be silly,' said Marcie. 'Nobody gives that sort of work to somebody our age.'

'It's supposed to be unofficial. He said I remind him of his little sister, who choked to death on pencil sharpenings.'

On pencil sharpenings! The Tulip touch! I was so mad at her for the sheer stupidness of it (and for ignoring me so horribly) that when she took a gold chain I'd never seen before out of her pocket and twirled it round her fingers, I left it to Marcie to ask all the questions.

'Where did you get that?'

'It's mine.'

'Is it gold, though? Real gold?'

'Of course it is.'

'Can I see it?'

'You're looking at it.'

'No, I mean, can I hold it?'

Pleased with her interest, Tulip spilled the chain into Marcie's hand. Marcie turned to the sunlight and studied it.

'This *is* real gold. It's got that funny mark.' She raised her eyes to Tulip's. 'It can't be yours.'

'Yes, it is.'

'I don't think so. It must be worth an awful lot.'

The edgy tone I knew so well came into Tulip's voice.

'Why shouldn't it be mine?'

Marcie said nothing, and, with Tulip standing there in her cheap clothes and worn jacket, there was no need.

Furious, Tulip snatched back the necklace and hurled it, glinting and rippling, as far as she could. It flew across the car park like a live snake, and fell with a rattle into the huge rubbish drum beside the wall.

We stared. Then Tulip said to Marcie,

'I don't want it any more. You can have it if you find it.'

Marcie hesitated just a shade too long. And then, humiliated by the notion of scrabbling in a dustbin for something cast out by Tulip, she turned her back on us.

'I don't want it!'

She strode away without another word. Part of me so longed to follow. I knew that I could catch her by the arm, and say to her, 'I reckon Tulip must have *stolen* that,' and in the sheer excitement of the moment, we could have become friends. I even thought that when she made up again with Claire, she very probably would let me stay.

I was still staring after her forlornly when Tulip said,

'I'm going home now.'

I walked with her as far as the bridge. We still weren't friendly. In fact, we hardly spoke. All I remember is that, at one point, she was struggling to find something at the bottom of her school bag, and things kept dropping, so she turned to me.

'Here,' she said. 'Be some help, will you? Hold my coat.'

Part Two

I

It was Julius who started it. We were sitting on the wall of the verandah one morning, poring over his spelling book, when he said suddenly,

'Did you know Tulip was a witch?'

'Don't be silly.'

'She is,' he said stubbornly. 'She always knows exactly what I'm thinking.'

'No one knows what you're thinking.'

'Tulip does.'

'Can we get on with these, please? *Wheelbarrow.*'

He reeled it off, 'W..h..e..e..l..b..a..r..r..o..w,' and went on without a break. 'She knew which cake I wanted yesterday. When Mum sent the plate round, Tulip was reading my mind to see which one I was after. Then she took it.'

'I expect you were staring at it.'

'No,' he said gravely. 'I used to be that silly. But I stopped doing that ages ago, and made it so I only *thought*.' He shifted uncomfortably on the ledge. 'Then she got good at that as well.'

'Good at what?'

'Knowing what I was thinking.'

'Julius –'

'And then,' he finished in a rush, 'I learned to make myself think something different. If I want the only coconut cake on the plate, I think "I want the chocolate one" as hard as I can. And, for a while, it fooled her.'

He laced his fingers, and bent them back nervously.

'But not any more. She can get through that too, now. She can read what I really think.'

And there was no shaking him. Tulip was a witch. And that's what must have set me off. From that day on, I lost my confidence that all the thoughts I had were quite my own. At first, it started as a little game. (Not one of the ones we did together. A private one I never shared with her.) I'd make believe that, if she wanted, she could read my mind, and even send her own thoughts directly into my head, to swirl about and make the whole place hers. I'd try and lay myself open to it, and be a blank slate in case it really could happen. And that felt so weird and puppet-like that I came to enjoy it. Soon, even when we were busy with other things, I'd secretly be playing *The Tulip Touch*, practically inviting her in.

'Want to play *All the Grey People*?' she'd ask me.

'Whatever you want.'

'I'll be the leader, shall I?'

'Yes. You be leader.'

'Right. First, we'll go through the coffee lounge. And then the writing room. And then the conservatory.'

'All right.'

You'd think I didn't have a will of my own. And wouldn't you suspect that she'd get bored, playing with such a servile shadow? But not a bit of it. It suited her fine. We'd march in silence through the chosen rooms, gazing with utter contempt at all those amazingly dull-looking people who spent an age tinkling their coffee cups, or staring into space over their drinks, or fiddling inside their handbags. Did they have any thoughts at all? Could they be thinking interesting things? Or were they just as they seemed – people with brains as grey and lifeless as their faces?

Dad spotted us on our third circuit.

'Okay, you two. Hop along. These rooms are supposed to be restful.'

And off we went, to play *Along the Flaggy Shore* in the upstairs passage, or *Fat and Loud* outside the bar. Whatever Tulip felt like doing next. She must have noticed I was different. But she never said a word. Even back then, that bothered me. What did she *think* was happening? And once I remember turning back, when she had sent me off across the hall to snaffle a few sheets of headed paper from the desk. And she had such a horrid smile on her face. Smug, she looked. Cocky.

I fetched the paper. But when I came back, my self-imposed reflex of submission failed.

'I don't see why *I* had to get it.'

'Oh, don't you?'

The tone was disdainful. And the look said, clear as paint: 'I know why you chose *me*. But surely, surely, even someone as stupid as you has worked out by now why it was someone like me chose *you*.'

2

Explain to me how you can come so close to rescue, only to have it snatched away. Just take the time when we were moving up together from the village school to Talbot Harries, in town. I didn't realize anything was brewing till Dad made a point of seeking me and Tulip out.

'So what are you two young ladies up to today?'

Tulip stood up and brushed the grass bits from her knees. We'd been in the middle of *Guest-stalk* (not one of the games we admitted to playing), and he'd blown our cover by walking straight up to us. Our prey strolled off.

'Nothing much. Why?'

'No reason.'

He gazed round, casually. It was quite obvious that he was after something, but not sure if he had the time to work it in the conversation gradually. Then one of the waiters appeared on the verandah to give him a quick 'You're needed in the restaurant' signal.

Dad came directly to the point.

'Which school are you moving on to after the holidays, Tulip? Is it Talbot Harries?'

She made a face.

'I suppose so. No one's said anything different.'

Now the waiter was back again. It was quite obvious there was a difficult guest inside.

'You'll still be with Natalie, then,' Dad told her cheerfully. And then, 'Excuse me, girls,' as he hurried back across the lawn. I couldn't look at Tulip. Suddenly, like someone drowning, I wanted so much to lift an arm to try and save myself. And Tulip could always read my face. If I knew Dad was lying, she'd know it too.

'Look at the peacocks,' I said. 'I hate the stupid way they walk.'

Tulip ignored me.

'If he's planning on separating us,' she said thoughtfully, 'he'll have to put more effort into it than that.'

That night, I overheard the plan.

'I think we should send Natalie to Heathcote.'

'To Heathcote? But *why*?'

'Why not? I know it's a lot further, but several children from the village go there.'

He saw me watching them and lowered his voice. Taking Mum's arm, he led her into the office. I didn't hear the rest. But over the next few days, Mum tried again and again to sound me out.

'How would you feel about it, Natalie? It's a long bus ride.'

I shrugged.

'You'd see a lot less of –' She hesitated. 'Some of your old friends.'

I shrugged again. I knew if I was sent to Heathcote, that would be curtains for mornings and evenings with Tulip. I'd set off too early and get back too late. It wasn't clear why it should make a difference to weekends. (It wasn't, after all, as if Tulip had hordes of admirers aching to step in and take my place.) But surely in a new school, with new teachers, new classmates, new people on the bus, I would be able to make new friends.

The registration forms sat in the in-tray on the reception desk. I fingered them over and over when no one was watching. *Heathcote Grange Secondary School. Last date for applications: Thursday 18th August.* I could have filled it in myself, it was so easy. *Name. Home address(es). Date of birth. Previous schools. Names and ages of siblings. Health problems (if any).*

The days before the deadline, I was a bird on a hot wire. Each time Dad came through a doorway, or cleared his throat, I was expecting him to say,

'Well, it's decided, Natalie. Heathcote, it is.'

On Monday, the wrong meat orders were delivered, and two of the waiters fell out and stormed off work. On Tuesday, Julius got a lump of grit in his eye, and rubbed it so hard he had to be taken down to the surgery. Wednesday was kitchen inspection. Everything stops for that. And on Thursday, though I hung around, wondering if Dad would suddenly come bounding down the steps ('You might as well see the place, Natalie. Why don't you come along for the ride?'), nothing happened. No one went anywhere. And when I fingered through the papers in the tray, I saw the form was still quite blank.

Tulip turned up next morning for the first time in a week. Dad met her on the stairs and suddenly looked troubled. She gave him her usual cheeky grin.

'Morning, Mr Barnes.'

'Hello, Tulip.'

Lightly, she bounced her fingers on the banisters, and carried on up. He hurried down. I watched him make for the reception desk and riffle through the in-tray.

Mum came out of the office.

'What's that you're looking for?'

He held it up.

'Oh, dear,' she said. 'Oh, what a nuisance! What's the date on it?'

'The eighteenth. Yesterday.'

'No point in driving it in, and begging them to take her anyway?'

He looked at his watch.

'The Newsams will be here in ten minutes to sort out the details of their wedding lunch.'

'I could do that with them.'

'I thought you were taking Julius for his check-up.'

'Oh. Right.'

There was a worried pause. I watched from overhead. Tulip was watching me. And suddenly I knew beyond a shadow of a doubt that she had stayed away all week deliberately, to lower their guard.

Mum shook off her unease.

'It's not too late, I'm sure. Shall we think about it as soon as we've got a free moment?'

Dad noticed Tulip lingering on the stairs.

'Yes. Later,' he said, and hurried off. And that was the last I heard. The form lay in the tray another week, and then it vanished. The last days disappeared as well. (We found a skylight with a smashed alarm, and played *Watch the Skies* behind the parapets.) And on the first day of

75

September I turned up at the bus stop. New journey. New uniform. New school. New set of teachers.

And good old Tulip, as usual.

3

I hated Talbot Harries. So did she. Hated the slime-green rooms, the shoving corridors, the ringing cloakrooms and the screaming bells. Hated the work, and hated the sarcastic teachers. Hated the food.

And hated being on my own. Someone had shopped us. We never found out if it was Dad, or the teachers from our old school. But we were separated for almost every lesson. Even our registration class was not the same. I'd catch a glimpse of Tulip as she was buffeted my way down some seething staircase, and call out hopefully,

'See you at break on the back steps!'

But she was hardly ever there, and each school hour went on for ever, till I was a bag of nerves who jumped at every raised voice in a corridor, and bit my fingernails until they bled, and couldn't concentrate on what the teachers said for hot tears prickling behind my eyes.

'This is your fault!' I shouted at Julius, when he caught me weeping over homework I couldn't do. 'If it weren't for you and your stupid sore eye, I'd be at Heathcote now!'

He backed away. I wondered if he'd gone to tell on me. But, no. He came back a few minutes later with a heap of mint imperials he'd pinched from the bowl in the coffee lounge. While I sucked for comfort, Julius patted me. And though it made it harder than ever to concentrate on the homework, I couldn't bring myself to shake him off. It wasn't Julius's fault that he was the apple of Mum's eye, and everything to do with him came first and second and next and last. Julius's tumbling class. Julius's visit to the clinic. New trousers for Julius. He didn't set it off, or even encourage it. Mum had no need of that. It hadn't escaped anybody's attention that even though furry rabbit and poor, battered Mr Haroun had long ago been tossed up on the shelf of precious cast-off cuddly things, Mum never did grow out of Julius. Even when he was dying to scramble out of the car, his fingers rattling the handle and his face turned to go, she'd be hungrily reaching out for him.

'Say goodbye properly, darling. Give Mummy one last hug.'

At least he never smirked or crowed at always coming first. Sometimes he even looked rueful, as if I'd been the luckier of the two, with no one noticing if I was there or not, or if I was happy, or if things were going right or wrong.

'Sorry,' I sniffled again. And he turned up the patting.

'I know,' he said. 'I'll go and tell them you're crying.'

It was a generous offer. It's never easy in a big hotel to get attention (if you're not paying for it). But if it was Julius who went, Mum would look up at once.

I shook my head.

'No. Honestly. I'll be all right.'

And no doubt I soon was. It's hard for anyone to start at a new school. Tiring and nerve-wracking. No wonder I was always so glad to see Tulip waiting on the steps at ten to four.

I'd rush up, full of questions.

'Where *were* you? You can't have been in your gym class. I went past twice, and didn't see you through the glass. Were you hiding in the cloakroom?'

She'd give her little sideways grin.

'Tell you later. Let's just get out of here.'

She'd take my arm, and off we'd go past all the people who'd come on with us from our old school. Susan and Janet, with their brand-new friends, and Will and Jamie, who'd been accepted at once in the 'Lads' Gang'. We'd saunter down the street towards our stop.

I'd hear a rumble gathering behind us.

'Here's a bus coming now.'

She'd cock her head to one side.

'What's it to be, then? Home or *Havoc*?'

And so relieved to be out of there, out at last, and no longer alone, I'd choose the one I knew she wanted to hear.

'*Havoc!*' I'd cry. '*Havoc!*'

And as the bus roared past, with the breeze of it whipping up our skirts, we'd slip away down the alley, out of sight.

4

You couldn't really call it havoc. It was just stupid things like cheeking people as we ran past, and telling old ladies their short cut was closed at the other end because the police had found a body with its throat cut, and hiding behind walls to flick mud pellets at women wearing smart jackets. ('Don't waste any of them on the men,' Tulip ordered. 'Men never bother, anyway.')

Sometimes we were spiteful. When the young mothers poured out of the playgroup centre into the post office shop, we'd stand in front of the display of foreign stamps till everyone's back was turned. Then Tulip would jam one of her specially selected twigs – short, but tough and sinewy – between the spokes of the nearest parked pushchair. Casually, we'd move into the queue, and watch with glee as the frustrated mother pushed and tugged, and struggled with the brake. Once, we watched one of them burst into tears, and I felt bad. But mostly I took Tulip's line on it. It was just 'fun', 'a good laugh', 'something to do'.

I only stopped her twice. Once, when she started with the milk bottle smashing. And another time, when she took someone's rabbit out of its hutch.

We'd had fun with animals before. Dead ones. It's not till you go looking that you have any idea how many dead birds and furry things are lying round the average town. (Sometimes I think I'll never be able to see another road kill without thinking of Tulip.) She'd flick them over with her shoe.

'Looks all right to me,' she'd say critically. 'Yes. That'll do.'

She'd scoop it up in one of the torn plastic bags with which Urlingham is littered, and we'd carry it round with us – it could have been a loaf and a pound of tomatoes – until we saw the perfect place.

'There's a hutch.'

We'd be up to the fence in a moment.

'Is it empty?'

'Doesn't matter.'

It wouldn't have, either. I'd watched her push fat, spoiled rabbits off their favourite patch of straw to shove a dead pigeon or blackbird in their place. But,

'I meant the *house*,' I said.

'Oh, that.' She glanced dismissively at the kitchen window with its prissy curtains hanging in scallops. 'There's no one looking, anyway.'

I checked the upstairs windows. But there were no signs of life, no shadows moving back and forth.

'Who's going, then?'

'I'll go.'

I gave her a leg up. There was no stopping Tulip once she'd started, so it was better to get the whole business done. She landed lightly on the other side. I passed the mucky bag over, and she set off boldly, sauntering across the lawn as if she owned it.

I watched her prise open the hutch lid.

'Well, hello, Thumper.'

She lifted the rabbit out by the ears. I hated that. I knew people said it didn't hurt them, but I didn't believe it. And there was something in the way she did it – slowly, deliberately, almost with relish – that set my nerves on edge, and started me scrambling along the fence, looking for a foothold of my own.

By the time I got over, she had her hands over its eyes.

'Gone dark, has it, Bunny?'

You had to be careful. She could turn just like that. So:

'Can I hold him, Tulip? Just for a little bit?'

She shook her head.

'First come, first served.'

'Please,' I said. 'Give him to me.'

She grinned unpleasantly.

'You don't know he's a he. He might be a she.'

'It doesn't matter. You could just let me have a go at cuddling him.'

'Only if you've guessed right.'

She upturned the squirming rabbit for no more than a couple of seconds.

'She's a she. So she's mine.'

'She's not *yours*, Tulip.'

'She is now.'

Tulip was crooning in the rabbit's ear. 'Who's a clever bunny? Who's going to be a good girl? Who's Tulip's special one? She's not going to make a fuss, is she? Oh, no. She isn't going to do that. Because she enjoys it really, doesn't she? And if she starts struggling, she'll get *hurt*.'

She finished up so savagely that I knew I was watching something horrible, nothing to do with the rabbit she was holding, but darker, much darker, and hidden, and coming from deep inside Tulip.

I heard my own voice saying,

'Put it *down*!'

It was like breaking a spell. The strange look cleared from her face. She practically threw the rabbit back on its straw, and turned away. I slammed the hutch lid closed.

'Quick!' I said. 'Someone's watching! Hurry up!'

She wasn't fooled. To prove it, she very deliberately took her time, snapping heads off the flowers as she strolled back towards the fence. I didn't care. I just scrambled over as fast as I could, and then, fuelled with relief at landing on the other side, gave myself over to her yet again.

'What shall we do now, Tulip? You decide.'

5

That was the year we started *The Little Visits*. I've no idea what set us off. All I remember is that one minute we were rollicking merrily, arm in arm, past some perfect stranger's front gate. And the next, we were on the doorstep, and Tulip had her finger pressed firmly on the ringing bell.

'Yes? Can I help you?'

I'm no good at ages. She was older than Mum, and younger than most people's grannies.

'We were wondering if you could tell us the way to the castle.'

'Castle?' The woman looked baffled. 'There's no castle round here.'

'Url Castle,' persisted Tulip.

It sounded so silly, I nearly let out a snigger.

'No. Not round here.'

But neither of us moved. And, in the end, she let us in the hall. While she leafed through a stack of pamphlets from a drawer, we rolled our eyes and made sneering faces at one another about the pictures on her walls.

'I'm sorry,' she said at last, looking up. 'I can find nothing here.'

But Tulip didn't move, so neither did I.

'You'll have to go now, I'm afraid,' the woman said after a moment.

I watched Tulip meet her gaze and willed her not to push her luck and get us into trouble. But then Tulip put on her false smile.

'Thank you for looking, anyway.'

Hastily, I slapped on my dad's be-pleasant-to-the-guests face.

'Yes. Thank you for looking.'

She was still staring when we turned at the gate.

'Goodbye,' Tulip called out sweetly. 'Thank you again.'

The woman didn't move. I wondered if somehow, by accident, Tulip had picked a particularly suspicious person, or if, at the next house she chose, there'd be somebody even more wary and watchful.

'Your turn,' said Tulip. She made me run up and down the street till my face was sticky and burning. Then I knocked on the door.

'Excuse me for bothering you. But could I please come in and have a glass of water?'

The elderly gentleman ran his eyes over my school uniform, as if to assure himself it wasn't fake.

'You needn't come in. I'll fetch some water. Just stay there.'

There was an edge to his voice, and he glanced round twice as he hurried to the kitchen. I knew if I so much as stepped over the wooden strip dividing indoors from out, he'd shoot back, whether or not the glass was filled, and order me away.

The tumbler he handed me was clouded and knobbly.

'There you are.'

He stood and waited. I took a couple of sips. Tulip had assured me that, if I could only get the person chatting, I'd be inside in a flash. So I said,

'We have some glasses just like this at home.'

'Do you?' he said coldly.

We don't, of course. The glasses at the Palace are crystal clear. Always shining. Always sparkling.

'Please hurry and drink it. I have things to do.'

I saw Tulip watching me from over the hedge.

'It's hard to drink fast,' I said hastily. 'The problem's with my throat. With swallowing. Last time I was in hospital, they thought they'd got rid of it. It's very unusual, you see, in someone my age. So everyone was very disappointed when it came back.'

And I was in, of course. I only stayed a few minutes, till I felt 'a little less dizzy'.

But I'd got in.

6

Gradually, over the months, Tulip set harder and harder tasks.

'May I please use your telephone?'

'Do you have a biscuit for my friend?'

'Would you lend me a pencil and some paper?'

It was astonishing, sometimes, just how easy it was. Some people didn't even count, said Tulip. They were obviously so lonely that if we'd been wearing masks and carrying knives, they'd still probably have ushered us into their kitchens. Others were bewildered or suspicious, which made it that bit harder to tack on the extras Tulip insisted on, like taking advantage of the house owner's back being turned to swivel a framed photo round to face the wall, or slide their scissors off the table and stab them, points down, in the soil of a plant pot.

We never stayed too long, though. Just in case. And, even so, I sometimes got home late. Usually, no one noticed. (It's not as if I walk through the main door and ask for my key at Reception.) But sometimes, slipping silently up the back stairs, I'd bump into Mum and see her glance curiously at her watch.

'Miss the bus, darling?'

'It was silly,' I'd say. 'Marcie and I got chatting, and then Mr Phillips wanted something carrying round to the laboratories, and . . .'

My voice trailed off, even before the next set of doors could swallow it entirely. She never called me back to hear the end. I doubt if she was listening, anyway. Always, in a hotel, there are dozens of things to get done. She was forever busy. And often I was glad of that. After Tulip invented *Wild Nights*, it might be hours before my heart stopped thudding, and I stopped being certain, each time the phone rang, that it was the fire service or the police.

I don't know why *Wild Nights* came as such a surprise. Tulip had always had a passion for fire. Candles, matches, sparklers, bonfires – she loved them all. I can't count the number of times Dad caught her behind the dustbins setting fire to paper just to watch it blaze and then flush with orange sprinkles as it crumpled to black at her feet. Give her some fancy wrapping paper, and she'd sit for hours tearing it into strips, and dropping them, one by one, into the fire in the back lounge.

'Look! Look at this greeny-blue!'

'Just like the peacocks' fans.'

Her face glowed with scorn in the firelight.

'No, no. It's much greener and bluer than that. These colours are *magic*.'

We helped with every bonfire. Well, I helped. She simply poked holes through the sodden leaves, and watched the red caves deep inside them burn.

'Come on, Tulip. I've fetched three whole bags while you've been standing there.'

'Ssh! Don't bother me.'

The gardener used to nudge me. 'Don't go too close,' he'd say. 'Can't you see Tulip's worshipping her fire god?'

It was a joke. But, honestly, you might have thought she was in church, the way she stayed so still, grave-faced and silent. Not like on *Wild Nights*. When we played that, some sort of unholy excitement ran through her every gesture, her every word. She'd push and pull me to the place she had in mind, while I begged not to go.

'Oh, please, Tulip. Let's just catch the bus straight home.'

'You're a coward and a lily-liver!' And sometimes worse. Once, a man passing by heard her swearing at me so foully, he stopped to stare.

She made a face at him, and pushed me on.

'We'll get in trouble,' I wailed.

'So?'

And I was quiet, because, for me, the notion of getting in trouble was so serious that I had to hide from her exactly how much it mattered. And she wouldn't have understood, anyhow. Things were so different at her house. Tulip said very little, but I'd picked up the fact that she was always being punished for stupid things like knocking a fork off the table, or leaving a stiff tap dripping a tiny bit, or not coming quickly enough when Mr Pierce called her. Her dad would suddenly let fly, and keep at her till even her timid mother was forced to stop pretending she hadn't noticed what was going on. She'd step in to try and stop him. Then Mr Pierce would turn his savage mood on her.

'It makes no difference what I do,' Tulip explained. 'He picks on me to start a fight with her.'

So there was no stopping her by wailing about 'trouble'. She simply grabbed handfuls of my coat, and pulled again.

'Come on, Natalie! It's all planned.'

Sometimes I'd trawl around for an excuse.

'No, not tonight. I promised Mum I'd help with next week's menus.'

Tipping her head to the side, she'd say sarcastically:

'Does the itsy-bitsy baby want to go home to her mummy?'

I hated it when she jeered at me.

'All right,' I said. 'But only something small.'

'A *Sweetie Swipe*?'

'No. He watches us every minute, Tulip. He *knows*.'

'All right, then. *Exploding Greenhouse*.'

'No!'

She made her last offer. '*Dustbin Fire*! It's only rubbish, anyway.'

'All right. A dustbin fire. But only *one*.'

'Only one.'

'Promise, Tulip.'

'Cross my heart.'

Her eyes went wide with honest promising, just as, in half an hour's time, they'd widen again from all the spitting orange magic conjured from some perfect stranger's matching grey bins.

'Tulip, you promised! *One*, you said.'

'I meant one *more*, Stupid!'

She was so horrid to me. Endlessly rude and disparaging. But, somehow, it didn't hurt. I think I just treated her insults like bad weather, keeping my head down, and pressing on with my self-appointed task of keeping her out of trouble. It was I who prised the package she was about to send to Mrs Bodell out of her hand.

'You can't post that!'

'Why not?'

'You're not allowed to put stuff like that in a letter box.'

I hurled it as far as it would go into the road, and watched with satisfaction as a car rolled over it.

'Good job I didn't bother with a stamp,' she said, unruffled.

In the same way, I confiscated her rude Christmas cards, one by one, as she finished them.

'Tulip, it's such a *waste*. You spend ages doing all this brilliant lettering, and I have to rip them into pieces and stuff them in the bin.'

'Nobody makes you.'

And it was true. Nobody made me. But still, somehow, I'd come to believe that keeping Tulip out of the trouble she spent her whole life fomenting was time well spent. And maybe it was, for me. It kept me close to her, and I needed Tulip. While I trailed round quietly, doing what I was told and being no trouble, Tulip lived my secret life. While teachers watched me sitting quietly at my desk, I was really outside on the hill with Tulip, openly watching the rest of us file in and out of classes. When I answered the Palace guests' boring questions over and over again, always polite, always smiling, I was secretly swearing as foully as she did. And when Mum didn't notice me as she swept past, looking for Julius, I was in silent rages that would put Tulip to shame.

I was as bad as she was, and the clever thing was, nobody even noticed. Even Dad was fooled.

'You're looking pale. Are you sure that you're sleeping properly?'

'I'm all right.'

He turned me round to the light.

'But you've got shadows underneath your eyes.'

'I've been doing a lot of homework.'

'Tell me another!' he scoffed. But you could tell that he believed me. And why not? It was a whole lot easier, and took less time, than trying to find out the truth.

7

Spring came, and Tulip's moods got worse and worse. She swung doors in my face, and kicked a huge dent in my cloakroom locker, and was so hateful that even I took to steering clear of her for days on end. Then I'd walk in the girls' lavatories to find her scratching foul words on the wall over the sinks. And just as if we'd never been apart, I'd be back to trying to stop her.

'Tulip, they've only just finished painting in here. What's the point of making it look horrible straight away?'

She gouged the plaster with her locker key.

'It's their own fault! They shouldn't have chosen such a vile colour!'

'What's wrong with it?'

'It's stupid, that's what. Pink! Pink for nice little girlies!'

'It's better than that old green.'

'I liked that green.'

'You said you didn't. You were always going on about it.'

Plaster sprayed from the wall.

'Oh, shut up, Natalie!'

She'd never had any patience, but now it seemed everything got under her skin. She was angry with everyone. And it didn't make any difference whether or not they were cross with her first. Almost as soon as anyone spoke to her, on went that little mask of frozen rage.

And when she wasn't angry, she was spiteful.

'That's rubbish, what you're drawing, Natalie.'

I kept my eyes on my paper. Apart from Games, when we were often ordered into separate teams, Art was the only lesson we had together now.

'At least I don't draw the same thing every week.'

And it was true. Give Tulip a piece of paper, and all she'd ever draw were children with huge, forlorn eyes copied from soppy greetings cards she'd lifted from the shop beyond the bus stop.

She moved her hand across to hide some now, because Mrs Minniver was coming our way.

'Have you started yet, Tulip?'

'I was just thinking first.'

Mrs Minniver inspected her watch.

'You've got exactly half an hour. By the time that bell rings, I want to see a proper painting. None of your usual little self-pitying cherubs up in one corner. Every inch of that paper must be covered. Now get on with it.'

Tulip turned to me sourly.

'So what is it?'

'What?'

'What we're supposed to be doing!'

'Self-portrait,' I said coldly.

'Really?'

It seemed quite genuinely to be news to her. And, peaceably enough, she lifted her brush and pulled my tray of paints nearer her easel than mine, to start with her careless brush stabbings and pokings.

'Aren't you going to draw yourself first?'

'I know what I look like.'

'But you'll go over the edges.'

'I'm not doing it with edges.'

I leaned across to see. She tugged her easel round, away from me. I went back to my own work. We sulked in silence for a little while. Well, *I* sulked. I think she just became absorbed in her painting. That horrid humming that she shared with her mother got on my nerves, but I didn't argue about it. I just kept hard at work, fretting about the face in my painting – too long, then too short, then too rubbed out and messy – till Kirstin strolled over to borrow a rubber and complain.

'That stupid Jeremy she's put me with! He's lost two of my rubbers already!'

'Well, look what I've got,' Tulip said contemptuously.

I looked up. She was pointing at me.

And did I rise up and hit her? Did I slap her face? Send her wobbly easel flying and pour the scummy brush water over her head?

No. I just said feebly, 'Oh, do shut up, Tulip!' and kept on with my work.

But I did hate her, then. I hated her so much that I could hardly wait for the half hour to disappear. I'd seen her fierce rubbings and scrubbings, her brutal daubs. Most people would take more care hurling rubbish in their dustbins. I'd seen her splayed brush come back again and again to the black, and what was left of the purple, and to the fiery red she'd turned to ditchwater with her careless rinsing. Suddenly I couldn't wait to see what Mrs Minniver made of Tulip's self-portrait.

The bell rang. She appeared in front of us.

'Finished?'

Tulip shrugged, totally indifferent, and tore her sheet of paper from the easel. Mrs Minniver took it from her. But though her face darkened as she inspected the painting, something about it must have given her pause, because she pinned it back on the easel and stepped back to look at it from further away.

And I stopped pretending that I wasn't watching, and looked at it too. It was the strangest thing. The fury and contempt of Tulip's brush work had turned to whirlpools of violence on the paper. Everything about it was dark and furious, and every inch of it seemed to suck you in and swirl you round, making you feel dizzy and anxious. And everywhere you looked, your eyes were drawn back, over and over, to the centre, where, out of the blackness, two huge forlorn eyes stared out as usual, half-begging, half-accusing.

I waited for the explosion. Would it be 'wasting paper' or 'dumb insolence'? Or, 'I *warned* you, Tulip. No more self-pitying little staring round eyes'?

But Mrs Minniver just said,

'*Look* at it. Now that you've finished, at least take a *look*.'

Putting her hands on Tulip's shoulders, she turned her to face the easel. Tulip's eyes went cold and hard. Mrs Minniver waited. But when it became obvious that Tulip wasn't going to say a word, she simply sighed.

'Well, then. Off you go,' she said gently.

Tulip reached out to rip the painting off the easel, but Mrs Minniver put out a hand.

'No. I'll keep this.'

Tulip stalked off. I stayed behind to pack her things along with mine, and ask,

'Will she get into trouble?'

Still staring distractedly at the painting, Mrs Minniver repeated,

'Trouble?'

'For making that huge mess,' I insisted. 'And doing more big round sad eyes, even though you told her that was exactly what she mustn't do.'

I don't know what I expected. But certainly not a look of such contempt.

I felt so frustrated and betrayed. I could practically feel myself screaming inside. *Why does Tulip always get away with it? Why does nobody ever stop her? Why? Why? Why?*

But the best I could manage to Mrs Minniver was a sullen:

'It was supposed to be a self-portrait. That's what you *said*. A self-portrait. Nothing else!'

I waited for her to tell me off. 'Disloyalty to a friend'. 'Making trouble'. But she just turned back to the painting.

'Oh, Natalie,' she said, as gently as she'd spoken to Tulip. 'Look at it. Just *look* at it.'

And this time it was there for me. My anger and frustration blew away like so much litter. I stood beside

Mrs Minniver, staring at Tulip's self-portrait, and this time all that I could think was what I finally managed to whisper.

'Oh, Mrs Minniver! I'm just so glad that I'm not her.'

8

So was it pity drew me back? Time and again, I'd almost gather up the strength to break away, and something would happen to stop me in my tracks. Like the day we heard the news about Muriel Brackenbury.

'Just think! We know somebody whose sister has drowned!'

'Tulip, stop *saying* that.'

'But we could sell our stories to the paper. We could be photographed with our arms around Janet.'

'Don't be ridiculous. Janet doesn't even like us.'

Tulip's eyes shone.

'I bet she's so upset. She won't be able to stop thinking about it.'

I was disgusted with her. Why was she so nosy about other people's feelings? Did she have none of her own, that she should be so obsessed about someone else's? And she didn't even feel sorry for Janet, that was obvious. She had the same look on her face as when we gave that horrible box to Jamie, and when she made Marcie cry by lying to her that she'd failed her maths. She just liked to prod and invent, and twist and poke, to watch people go ugly with fright, or burst into tears of misery.

Now she was rolling Muriel's name round and round.

'Brackenbury. Brackenbury. It's odd, isn't it? Because, I expect, when she was found, she was near bracken. And near berries.'

'If you don't stop talking about it, I'm catching the next bus home.'

She didn't even hear me.

'Drowned! Think of it. To get so close to the bank, and still go under. Swallowing all that water. I expect Janet will keep waking up imagining it now. I bet she will. After all, it's her sister.'

'Don't, Tulip! It's *horrible*.'

'Yes, isn't it?'

I stared at her. She thought I meant 'horrible to drown', not 'horrible to say'. And settling herself on the wall by the bus stop, she just went on and on.

'It must feel awful, opening your mouth for air, and more and more water rushing in instead. I expect you swallow so much that, when they find you, you're all swollen up. Not like with kittens. I bet a person must keep trying, over and over, to –'

But I'd stopped listening. Everything round us – the street, the cars, the people – all bleached away to invisible. And I was back to eight years old, holding my father's hand on a baking afternoon, and seeing Tulip for the very first time, still as a stone in that cornfield.

Not yet a friend of hers. Not yet sucked in. And not in the slightest scared of her.

'You *drowned* that kitten, didn't you?'

She broke off her excited ramblings.

'Which kitten?'

'The one you were holding on the day we met. I always thought it was your dad who got rid of them. But it was *you*.'

'No, it wasn't.'

She said it quite firmly, though it wasn't true. But I was used to that. And suddenly I understood how Tulip could lie and lie, and never see how ridiculous her untruths looked to other people. In her eyes, it was the *world* that was wrong. If the world had only been right, if things had only fallen out the way they should, then she would never have had to lie, or steal, or be spiteful. If the world had only been right, she'd be a nice and good person – the girl she was inside, before it all went wrong, and she got spoiled all along with it.

'It *was* you,' I persisted.

'So what if it was?'

'Nothing.' I kept my voice easy, even bright. 'I was just wondering, that's all.'

'Wondering what?'

'What it was like.'

She turned to look at me. I forced myself not to show even a flicker of feeling. I closed my mind to her. Slam! Clang! Shutters down! I wasn't going to play *The Tulip Touch* right now.

'It's none of your business.'

'I know,' I said. 'It's just that I never realized. And you never said.'

She gave the flippant playground retort.

'You never asked.'

I felt like screaming at her, 'Why should I *ask*, Tulip? Whoever would have even *thought*?' But, instead, I walked my fingers steadily along the wall, and tore off a strip of moss.

'Did it take long?' I asked, casually pulling the shreds apart.

Can you sense truth coming? Oh, I think you can.

'That's why I always had to do it myself,' she said, firm, proud, self-righteous, even. 'So it would take less time. They had to be done, you see, or we'd be *overrun*.' I knew it was her father's word from the way that she said it. '*Overrun*. But Dad wouldn't take the time. He'd just shove them in a crock of water and slam the lid, and you could hear them scrabbling and pushing at the top. And it took forever.'

I bet it did. I could hear it as I sat listening. The mewings and scratchings. The lid lifting like potatoes on the boil. The driblets of water down the side of the crock that only let in more air to prolong the struggle.

All her cocky self-confidence had drained away. She said so sadly:

'It took hours and hours.'

I passed her half my moss. It sat on her skirt in a crumbling lump, but she didn't push it off.

'I did try to stop him. Once I even went at him with a fork. But he just laughed, and called me "another little cat who could do with a ducking". He didn't even bother to wallop me.' (Even after all this time, she sounded a little surprised.) 'He just threw me out of the house, and rammed home the bolt. Then he sat with his feet on the table, reading the paper, and I had to watch through the window. It took hours and hours.'

Her spongy bitten fingertips scrabbled for comfort in the moss.

'Not *hours*,' I consoled her. 'Kittens wouldn't be strong enough. Honestly. Not hours.'

'Long enough,' she said. 'So ever since then I've always done it myself. Because it's quicker. And once they're under, I never let them up again.'

I put my arm around her. No wonder she was so interested in Muriel Brackenbury's horrid death. If someone else had known the horrors of all those thrashings and struggles, and beads of air glistening to the surface, maybe she wasn't so alone.

I slid off the wall. Taking her hands in mine, I tugged at her gently.

'Come along, Tulip. Time to go home.'

Then, one day, I heard the office staff discussing her.

'What *has* that child done with her hair?'

'Which?'

'Tulip Pierce.'

I rooted deeper in the chest of lost property, hiding my face.

'Oh, *Tulip*.'

They stared out of the window in silence for a while. Then one of them said,

'She is a strange one, that's for sure.'

Her colleague sniffed.

'I can't be doing with her. Bold and sassy if you speak to her. But the minute she wants something from you, she turns into Miss Cute & Mincing.'

'Have you seen her fingernails? They're bitten raw.'

'I can't *think* what she's done to her hair. It looks as if someone's been at it with the garden shears.'

The phone began ringing, and the nearest one turned from the window.

'My sister knows the mother,' she remarked. 'Just through her dealings with the farm.' She reached out to press the flashing red button. 'She says she always gets the feeling that one day she might start screaming and never stop.'

I wondered who she meant. Tulip's mother? Or Tulip? And was this what the painting was about? Was this why Mrs Minniver, and everyone else, treated Tulip as if she were as dangerous as one of her own dustbin blazes?

Poke a fire, and it flares more fiercely. Everyone knows that.

The only safe thing is to stay away.

I think I almost came to the decision then. And maybe a dozen other times when I stepped out in early morning air, and knew I couldn't face her. On those days, I'd skip school myself, and spend the hours hiding in the Palace's abandoned laundry, where my footfalls raised puffs of dust, and I had to sit uncomfortably amid tubs and basins, in the shadow of a giant old mangle, watching a frill of light creep under the door.

At four o'clock, I'd make my way, out of sight, around the Palace to the bus stop. After a day in oily gloom, the great bars of sunlight sweeping so cleanly over the fields made me feel tearful and giddy.

I'd make sure Tulip was nowhere in sight.

Then I'd walk home, as usual.

Tulip wore black until it was taken from her.

'The colour for sweaters in this school is *blue*.'

'But I'm wearing black for Muriel.'

'Muriel?'

'Muriel Brackenbury.'

You could tell that the teachers were disgusted. 'Self-indulgence stretched into morbidity,' said Mrs Powell. Mr Hapsley gave her a detention each time he saw her. And as soon as Miss Fowler was told, she stormed down the stairs from her office.

'Take off that pullover. It's confiscated.'

'But I don't have another one with me.'

'That's your problem, Tulip. Maybe tomorrow you'll wear proper uniform.'

I found her waiting at the bus stop, shivering.

'Why didn't you go straight home?'

'I can't. I daren't. She said she'd be phoning my father.'

So that's how I came to go on my last *Wild Night*. This time, it was a shed a mile out of town. I don't know where she'd got the paraffin. Maybe she'd sneaked it from home. I can't believe the people who owned that chicken farm were stupid enough to leave three whisky bottles filled with paraffin in a ditch on their own land.

'Tulip –'

'Ssh! If you can't help, at least don't spoil things by fussing.'

'Are you quite sure the shed's empty?'

'You *know* it's empty. We've walked through it twice. Now pass me the last bottle.'

The shed went up like nothing I've ever seen. Huge flames licked the sky, and smoke billowed up like a giant black genie freed from a bottle after thousands of years. The fire roared and crackled. Rafters collapsed like straws. And the dancing sparks spat and hissed as, one by one, the empty racks seethed and frizzled.

But this time it was Tulip tugging at my arm.

'Natalie! Natalie!'

I shook her off. The only thing I wanted was to stand and watch this great orange dragon leap higher and higher.

'Natalie! Quick, or we'll get caught! The police always suspect everyone standing and watching!'

But, though she pulled at me, I wouldn't budge. Why go to all the trouble to raise a fire, and then not stay and watch? All round that chicken farm were hedges and hawthorn trees and clumps of bushes. If she'd been here before to stuff her bottles of paraffin into the ditch, surely she could have found some place we could have hidden. Why take so many risks, then walk away from all the glorious, spell-binding magic you've created? Why miss the fizzing, crackling glory of something so plain and drab exploding into fireballs and shooting stars?

'Oh, please, Natalie! Please!'

She tugged so hard at me, I had to go. But as I stumbled after her, still looking back, I knew I was bewitched. *The Tulip Touch* had really got me this time. I knew I'd dream of fires for ever, and wake in the middle of my dull, dark nights to see the flames she might have lit in me still shooting up to scorch the sky. I'd see whole streets, entire cities, burning. I'd switch on my bedside light and, for a while, the old familiar pictures on the walls and clothes on the chair might blot out the smouldering visions. But I'd be sure Tulip was lying waiting in some bleak bedroom. And I'd know the minute my room was dark again, she'd pick up where she left off, and send more of her own imaginings into my boring dreams, to set them ablaze with her own growing frenzies.

'Natalie? Natalie! Are you all right?'

I heard the whine of a siren. Was it in my head, or coming from across the field?

'Down here. Quick!'

She pushed my head below the level of the ditch, and stayed close behind me as we crept along.

'See that gap? That one!'

I crawled through the tiny hole in the hedge. She followed, and we lay on our backs, panting. I still felt dizzy and strange. And then, suddenly, out of the whirl of confusion came the first inklings of other, darker, more destructive visions.

And slowly, slowly, I came to my full senses at last.

Is it like this for everyone? Is it unusual to have your life bowling along steadily in one direction, and then, in a flash, change utterly? Change *everything*. For those were the moments when our friendship died. It's as easy as that to pin down. Oh, I let her rattle on, lifting her head to look at the fire engines, working out which way we ought to go back to the bus stop if we weren't to be noticed, talking excitedly about how fast that old wood flared up and burned. But all the time I was thinking, people *hide* in sheds. I'd spent whole days in the abandoned laundry. If someone I didn't know had walked through, I would have held my breath in the shadow of the huge, rusting mangle. And in the tension of the moment, even someone with hearing as good as mine might not have noticed the soft suspicious splatter of liquid on old trampled straw.

And what about Julius? He had a dozen dens. So did his friends. They hid for hours in outhouses so frail and rotten that, under the ivy that held them together, they would flare up in a moment.

Was Tulip *mad* as well as bad?

I clambered to my feet, and held out my hand as usual to pull her up.

'Come on, Tulip. Time to go home.'

On the bus, she was her old, cocky self, flirting with the driver and slyly tipping people's shopping bags over with her feet.

Halfway back, she got restless.

'Want to play *All the Grey People*?'

'Sure,' I said. And I did a good job of pretending all the way. But when you've just won the hardest game of all, the others lose their colour. And so my heart wasn't in it, and it fell flat.

From the bus stop, we walked together to the bridge.

'Well,' I said cheerfully. 'See you tomorrow.'

'Why don't I come as far as the Palace?'

I gave her a long look. She really hadn't realized I was out of it. She didn't know that she could never recast the spell.

'If you like,' I said.

We strolled arm in arm up the drive. I felt quite calm. I wasn't worried in the least. And that, in itself, felt strange. It seemed that, from the day we'd met, I'd been in thrall to Tulip. Everything I'd said, everything I'd done, had her in mind. Like a tongue to a wobbly tooth, my every thought had come straight back to her. I had become a shadow to my parents. I'd floated out of reach of Julius. I had no friends. I hadn't been there for anyone, except for Tulip.

And it was over. All over.

I let her walk with me as far as the last bend in the drive. Then, as the Palace came in view, I broke away, and dropping my school bag, I ran as fast as I could across the rose garden, under the archway, and down the narrow twisty path snaked over with tree roots.

I heard her calling. 'Natalie! *Natalie!*' But I didn't answer. I just ran. *Stay away from fire.* And when I'd reached the middle of the thicket, I came off the path and dived into the bracken.

I crawled and crawled. While she was thrashing between the trees, I'd make a little progress. Then when she was perfectly still, cunningly waiting, I didn't move at all.

'Natalie! *Natalie!*'

She was beating so fiercely at the undergrowth with a stick that I got a little further under the cover of her noise.

And then even further, till I had reached our old mud slide. And down I went, down, down, sideways like a rolling log, faster and faster, until I came to rest in the very deepest bracken.

And there I lay, grinning up at the fronds that had closed over my head. She'd never find me now. I was safe in the green dark of jungle, of deep, deep, sunless pools. I lay on my back and listened as she called.

'Natalie! *Natalie!* Come out, stupid! It's raining!'

The first few drops pattered through the whispering fronds. The dripping turned into trickles, but I didn't move. Let her call. Let her search for me.

Let her give up and go home.

A soft bead of rain ran over my forehead and in my ear, and I recalled Miss Golightly, years before, explaining a picture in Assembly.

'He's pouring the water over the baby's head to put her on the side of light.'

Tulip crashed nearer, but my heart stayed steady.

'Go away,' I willed her silently, playing *The Tulip Touch* backwards for the very first time. 'Turn around. Go away. I don't want you anywhere near me.'

Not fire. *Light.*

She called a few more times, ever more hopelessly.

And then she left.

Part Three

Part Three

It was like coming out of hospital. You don't get straight back into being yourself. It takes a little time. And just as someone with a broken foot gingerly tests it each morning to see how much pressure it can take, I stretched things a little further every day.

I had to be careful with Tulip. She was on her guard.

'What happened on Friday? Why did you run off like that?'

'Oh, I'm sorry. I suddenly felt so queasy. I knew I couldn't make it back to the Palace, so I ran off between the trees.'

'Didn't you hear me calling?'

'I was *sick*.'

The next day, she wanted to come home with me.

'We've got workmen,' I told her. 'And Dad says he doesn't want any extra visitors.'

'What about the weekend?'

'There's a special wedding party.'

'We could stay out of sight.'

'No, Tulip.'

She gave me a suspicious look. I knew how odd it must have sounded to her. She'd never heard me saying no before.

'You're hiding something, Natalie.'

'No, I'm not.'

'Well, something's going on. I used to be able to come, even when there were special parties and weddings.'

I let the same look of dumb insolence spread over my face as I'd seen so often on hers.

'Well, that was last year, Tulip.'

At this reminder of the game we used to play, she turned on her heel and walked off. I went back to my classroom, grinning. And it was only then I realized that, in this small daily probing of sides of myself left too long untested, I'd come across a few things I'd totally forgotten. The feeling of power. The sense of being in control.

Mr Scott Henderson was the first one to notice she was never around.

'Where's your friend Tulip these days? Have you two had a little spat?'

I looked unconcerned and lied glibly (both skills I'd learned from her).

'Not really. She's got other friends.'

And soon she had. First she took up with Marcie once again, though that lasted only till the craze on playing cards began in break time. Then Marcie got fed up with Tulip's habit of going on about the rules through every hand, and telling everyone what they'd done wrong, and gloating over winning.

'It's just a game,' she said. 'It doesn't *matter*. Why do you care so much?'

Tulip's eyes flashed, and she stormed off. And after that she was alone again, till someone called Heather came down from Scotland and started at Talbot Harries. Like me, all those years ago, she didn't know any better than to offer her friendship to the first person she saw standing alone. And for the next few days I had to watch Tulip grin at me contemptuously, and turn her back, and giggle in corners with Heather.

But that didn't last, either. Heather soon took against Tulip's mean habit of eating the sweets she always had in her pocket without offering them to anyone round her. And Tulip's 'joke' of tipping the contents of Heather's lunchbox into the bin, and filling it with dirt and stones, fell very flat. So Heather soon made other friends. In any case, watching the two of them walk round together, arm in arm, hadn't made me unhappy. All I could see was how foolish I must have looked when it was me. All I could feel was sheer relief.

That was the strangest thing about those weeks: the feelings that I had. Like coming out of a grey, endless dream, I felt the world lift around me. For far too long, I'd stayed in Tulip's shadow. Each day now, I felt a bit stronger and things went better. At school, because I wasn't looking out for her on every staircase and through every window, my work was more careful and my marks improved. At the Palace, I walked more briskly in and out of rooms, no longer endlessly hovering by windows and doorways to see if Tulip was coming. Without half my brain engaged in waiting for her, I became a whole person again. At night I still dreamed of fires, and woke in frights. But in the day, so different did I feel, so little did I want to be the Natalie I was before, that I'd have changed my name if they'd have let me. And on the morning I found myself sitting peacefully on the ledge of the verandah, watching the peacocks instead of – one of the games she'd taught me – stalking them till they panicked, I realized for the first time in years that I was happy.

Happy.

And that's why, when Julius ran round the corner to tell me Tulip was waiting in the rose garden, I didn't want to know.

'Go back,' I said, 'and tell her you can't find me.'

'Why?'

'Because I don't want to see her.'

'But what about Tulip? If you're not with her, the gardener will tell her to go home.'

I slid off the ledge and moved towards the door.

'Just tell her I can't come. Say that I'm busy helping Dad.'

He looked baffled. But then he shrugged, and ran back the way he'd come. I felt a little bit guilty, but not much. Staying away from Tulip was getting easier each day.

And I avoided her at school as well. Skills learned in *Guest-stalk* came in useful now.

'Coming, or going, Natalie?'

I'd step aside to let the teacher pass. I didn't know yet, did I? If she was outside, I was staying in. If there was no sign of her, then I might slip out between the wide glass swing doors.

I'd have my bag packed by the end of school. I'd hare up Forest Street, though it was further, to catch the bus one stop ahead. I'd keep my head down as it roared past the gates, in case she was standing there waiting, or trailing her bag towards our usual stop in the vain hope I'd catch her up and keep her company. It wasn't my fault that she was alone. Nobody forced her to shove people so hard they fell, and splatter ink on their clothes, and call out 'Cheap

Scottish Heather!' all the time at someone who'd tried to be friendly.

Each time she came to the Palace, Julius told me off.

'You can't just keep saying you're busy.'

'Yes, I can.'

'You can't. It's mean. Tulip's supposed to be your friend.'

'Just tell her I've gone to Urlingham with Mum. That's not so difficult, is it?'

'It's not that it's difficult,' said Julius. 'It's just that I feel sorry for her.'

'Well, don't!' I snapped. 'It's just a trap!'

He stared at me as if I'd bitten him.

'What do you mean?'

'Nothing,' I said, getting a grip again. 'I didn't mean it.'

But I did. I was *sick* of feeling sorry for Tulip. I felt she'd caught me young, and sucked me in, and even made me bury my own feelings so deep, I practically didn't have them. She'd kept me down with her contempt and scorn. But things were different now. It was my turn to feel contempt. And I think I must have realized that part of my growing strength came from despising her, because I didn't stop at my new disapproval of her mad habits and her crooked ways. I took it a step further. Now, when we met in the corridors, I'd smile, and say hello, and mutter something about meeting at break. But at the same time,

I'd be taking care to glance at the great lumpy hems on her second-hand school skirt, with all the ugly stitching showing through, or at the ragged hair she cut herself, so I could will myself to think:

'You're nothing, Tulip. *Nothing.*'

Oh, it was horrible. It was to save my life, but I could *weep*.

2

She never asked me what was wrong again. Sometimes I found my locker filled with litter, or my name on the 'Commendation List' scratched out so hard it gouged the paintwork on the corridor wall. But I kept quiet about it to the teachers, and never said a word at home.

Still, even my parents must have noticed she never came. So I was really surprised when, halfway through December, Dad lifted his head from the Christmas seating plan to say to me,

'I take it Tulip's coming, as usual?'

I couldn't work it out at all.

'I'm not inviting her,' I said.

He and Mum exchanged glances. Mum fiddled with the gold chain round her neck.

'But you know how much Tulip loves Christmas.'

'I love Christmas as well,' I said stubbornly. 'And I don't feel like inviting her this year.'

They looked uneasy. I got the feeling Dad was on the verge of telling me something, but, at a look from Mum, he changed his mind. Instead, he just said mildly,

'But she doesn't have much of a life, does she? So it might be nice.'

Inside, I was seething. So that was it! I'd fought so hard to get free, yet here were both of them quite ready to throw me back, just to ease their own guilty consciences. They knew as well as I did she hadn't been in the Palace for weeks. But how could they feel as Christmassy as usual, if Tulip wasn't there, to make them feel even more giving and generous, with Dad feeding her titbits, and Mum whispering to the guests.

'Oh, yes. She has a pretty thin time of it at home. So we do try to give her at least one really special day.'

Well, they couldn't have it both ways.

'Let Julius invite her,' I said slyly. 'She's really more his friend now.'

'Julius?'

Mum was so startled, she almost snapped the necklace.

'Yes,' I said. 'They spend quite a bit of time together now. They're thick as thieves.'

'Julius? And *Tulip*?'

Dad put his hand on Mum's to calm her down.

'I've never noticed,' he said suspiciously.

'You're always very busy.'

He let it drop. But Mum soon slid away to have a quiet word with Julius. I don't know what he said. But why should he have hidden the fact that, if he noticed Tulip on his way home from school, or saw her hanging round the edge of the cornfield, he always ran across to say hello? After all, he felt *sorry* for Tulip.

Didn't they all?

So my mean little plan to protect myself worked like a charm. Mum might not bother all that much about me, but when it came to looking after precious Julius, no one else stood a chance. The very thought of having Tulip for Christmas slipped out of everybody's mind, and no one said another word.

Except Mr Scott Henderson. At the piano on Christmas Eve, he poked me gently in the ribs.

'Are you missing her?'

'No,' I said sourly, not even bothering to pretend I didn't know who he meant.

'I do,' he said. 'I've always had a soft spot for your little friend.'

'She's not so little,' I said. And then I thought of something cleverer. I put on a more pleasant face and turned to beam up at him.

'I could explain to you how to get to her house. Then, since you're so fond of her, you could go and visit.'

That shut him up. He made great play of flicking through his carol sheet. Then, when the singing started, he kept his head bent to the words as if he didn't know them, and never caught my eye again.

I sang out, missing Tulip horribly, and hating them all. Why should they assume she was my job, always *my* job? They all knew where she was. They knew that she'd be sitting in her drab everyday clothes, listening to her mother hum and her father nag as she fingered some horrid cheap present scrimped from what was left of the housekeeping after Mr Pierce finished buying his booze. They all stood round the piano, so smug, so stuffed with food and so dolled up. What was so wrong with one of *them* filling a hamper and taking it over? Or even bringing her back with them? 'Come on, Tulip. We know you're not best friends with Natalie any more. But *we* still care about you. Come with us.'

But, no. That was *my* job. Look after Tulip (but don't be her hold-your-coat merchant). Be nice to her (but mind you don't get sucked in too far). Go play with the witch (but don't let her cast any spells on you).

Oh, dream on.

3

Did she sit there expecting us till the very last minute? ('Jump in, Tulip! Christmas is Christmas, after all.') Because, after that, there was no more pretending. When we met on the school stairs, she flashed me such a look of hate, and I stared past her coldly.

And with no friends, she went from bad to worse. I heard the whispers almost every day. 'Did you know about Tulip? Guess what she's done now!' She hardly came in to school. And when she did, she had an air of smouldering anger around her. The boys picked up on it straight away, calling her 'Crazy Tulip' until the strange frozen mask on her face cracked, and she turned wild, and spun into frenzies of violence that had the phones ringing and the male staff running.

In February, she was banned from Harry's Supermarket. A few weeks after that, the police came in to school on her account. No one was sure exactly what it was about, but I realized I'd not known how much trouble she'd been in till I heard some of the guesses.

'It'll be because of those windows.'

'Don't be soft. The police don't come round for smashed windows. Maybe she had the nerve to go back to Wilkins Hardware.'

'To nick the batteries she forgot?'

They all laughed. I turned away, embarrassed, because even after all these months of steering clear of her, some of them still thought of me as Tulip's friend. And so did most of the teachers. Because it was to the Palace that the police were sent that very same night, pulling their caps off as they walked through the door, but ignoring the curious glances from the guests on the sofas.

Mum hurriedly ushered them away from Reception, and through the door into the office.

'You stay here, Natalie,' she said. 'Watch the desk for me, will you?'

The woman officer stood back to let me pass. But the man said,

'I think we might sort things out quicker if the young lady comes in as well.'

'Really?' Mum was astonished. But she didn't argue. Instead, she called George in from the bar, and asked him to find someone to cover Reception.

'Now,' she said, closing the door behind us all. 'What's all this about? How can I help you?'

But they weren't to be hurried.

'Maria Benson,' said the woman, offering her hand to Mum.

'Stallworthy,' said the other, and smiled, though he made no effort to shake hands.

They glanced at the chairs till Mum said, 'Please do sit down.' And then they seated themselves, and looked at me. But I'd learned the blank face from Tulip. I didn't flinch.

'It's about some little visits,' said the woman officer.

My heart began to thump. How long can your old life follow you? We couldn't have played *Little Visits* for nearly a year.

Mum was mystified. 'Little visits?' She turned to me. 'What little visits?'

I was so lucky. Before I could put my foot in it, Officer Benson broke in again, to try and explain.

'You see, we're having a little problem with Tulip Pierce.'

'Oh, Tulip!' Mum's relief was evident. 'Tulip! I might have known!'

'And we were wondering if Natalie here could help us understand.'

I watched them warily, but it was Mum who asked.

'Understand what?'

'Why on earth she might be doing what she's doing.'

Mum looked from one to the other.

'And what's that?'

The policeman picked at his cap. He seemed embarrassed suddenly, and tired.

'We've had a complaint. It seems Tulip has made three little visits to the family of that poor girl who drowned a while back. She keeps coming up to Mrs Brackenbury's door, and knocking, and asking her –'

He stopped, and seemed, for a moment, to be inspecting the plasterwork on the ceiling.

'Asking her –?' Mum prompted.

He took a deep breath.

'Asking if Muriel would like to come for a walk.'

I saw Mum wasn't understanding yet. So did the officer. He tried again.

'Muriel Brackenbury,' he explained. 'The girl who drowned.'

Mum's face went ugly with disgust.

'Tulip is *visiting* them? And asking after their dead child?'

'Standing there on the doorstep.'

'Grinning all over her face.'

'But that's disgusting! That's horrible! That is the worst, the sickest –'

She turned her anger and revulsion on me.

'Do you *hear* this? I hope I never again hear of you spending time with Tulip Pierce! Do you understand what these officers are *saying*?'

Officer Stallworthy broke in.

'That's why we're here, Mrs Barnes. Because –' He hesitated, perhaps fearing to focus Mum's wrath onto any particular gossips. 'Because, when we asked around, we heard that Natalie may know Tulip well enough to help us understand exactly what it is we're dealing with here.'

Mum's eyes were flashing.

'You want to know if Tulip's mad, or bad?'

His tired and embarrassed look came back again.

'That's not how we'd put it, of course. But if your daughter –' He turned to me. 'Natalie, can you help us out? Can you tell us what's going on here?'

Oh, I did an excellent job. I looked so puzzled and anxious. I got more and more distressed. I shook my head, and started sentences I couldn't finish. And they must have thought I was being as open and honest as I could. You could see it on their faces. 'This girl is doing her level best to be some help.'

But all I let them know, through my pathetic stammered confidences, was that I'd stopped being friends with Tulip months ago, even before she took up with Marcie, and, afterwards, with Heather. Everyone could tell them that, I

136

said. They could check it. But I told them nothing that they needed to know. I hadn't spent all that time building a wall between the old Natalie and the new to take it down now, for these two. So I never even tried to explain what was quite clear to me. Perfectly obvious.

If I'd been inventing games for two my whole life, and suddenly my old partner refused to play, what would there be to do but think up a whole load of new games, just for one?

And what a game! Here was I thinking our *Little Visits* had been so cool, so risky. And what was Tulip doing? Walking up to the mother of a dead girl and asking if her daughter could come out for a walk! Not just once, but three times in a row!

I was awestruck. She'd really left me standing, hadn't she? Here was I, playing Little Goody Two Shoes with Mum and Dad, and passing tests at school, and even spending hours with Julius. And here was she . . .

And once again I saw the old bewitching vision of how things could have been. The constant beat of excitement. Her hand in mine. And flickering, rising colours. Colours to light the sky, and warm my grey, grey soul, and fill my dreams for ever.

But standing there grinning, they'd said. Grinning all over her face.

At Muriel Brackenbury's *mother.*

Other people's feelings aren't dice, or counters.

'*Three times!*'

Officer Stallworthy took my belated disgust for astonishment, because he said a bit defensively:

'Well, naturally, the first time, the Brackenburys thought it must be some horrible mistake.'

'As anyone would,' said Mum tartly.

'As anyone would,' he repeated. 'It was only the second time that they rang us.' He paused. 'And we made the same mistake. We just assumed that someone had got the wrong end of the stick. Upsetting, of course. But totally innocent.'

Again, he stared at the ceiling.

'But then, this evening –'

This evening! Incredible! Less than three hours ago I'd spotted her from the bus as it swept past school. She'd looked the same as usual. But here were these two police officers saying she'd strolled up the path to a house (where, for all she knew, half of the county's squad cars were lying in wait for her after her first two visits) and treated another human being as if she were just part of some *game*.

'She's mad,' said Mum. 'There has to be something wrong with her. She's insane.'

Officer Stallworthy decided the visit was over. He took a card from his breast pocket, and after hesitating between Mum and me, put it in my hand.

'Any time,' he said gently. 'Anything you can think of that might help. Anything at all.'

I nodded.

They moved towards the door. Mum signalled me to stay behind, but still I distinctly heard her say,

'Honestly, I don't know what Natalie ever saw in Tulip Pierce.'

Perhaps it was her dismissive tone that irritated Officer Stallworthy. Maybe, if you're in the police, you get a little tired of people in plushy surroundings telling you how they're above all the squalid little messes you spend your whole life sorting out.

Anyhow, he said rather coldly:

'Perhaps, Mrs Barnes, it's time to start wondering just what it was that Tulip saw in Natalie.'

Mum just ignored the jibe. But to remind him who was supposed to be the villain here, she asked,

'And what is likely to happen to Tulip now?'

'Oh, we'll speak to her. She won't go bothering them again.'

The wall I'd built so carefully broke. Not even caring that Mum would realize I'd been eavesdropping, I rushed through the door and caught him by the sleeve.

'Promise me you won't tell her father! Promise me!'

Mum looked first shocked, then disapproving.

'They'll have to speak to Tulip's parents, Natalie.'

'No! Please!' I begged. 'They mustn't! If they tell Mr Pierce, he'll *kill* her. I *know* he will!'

Officer Stallworthy said kindly,

'Don't you worry. We'll take it very gently. I think we all know about Mr Pierce's temper.'

'No!' I cried, dragging at him, near hysterical, half dead with fright for Tulip. 'You don't understand. If you tell him what she's been doing, he'll half murder her. He'll just be glad to have the chance. He'll sound reasonable enough while you're there. But the minute you're gone –'

The words came searing back from games we'd played together, things she'd said.

'The minute you're gone, he'll thrash her like a redheaded stepchild! He'll whip her till her freckles sing!'

They stared at me, appalled. Even my mother was silent.

The officers eyed one another, said nothing, and were gone.

4

News travels fast in a hotel. Mum didn't say a word to me, but she must have spoken to someone, because the very next evening I walked through the lounge to hear the argument raging around me.

'Wickedness!' Miss Ferguson was saying. 'Pure *wickedness!*'

'Nonsense,' said Mrs Pettifer. 'The child is obviously deeply disturbed.'

Instead of moving on through the double doors, I drifted to a halt out of sight behind one of the pillars, to listen. As usual, Mr Enderby tried to keep the peace.

'It might have been a misunderstanding. That's always possible.'

'Oh, really!' snapped Miss Ferguson. 'It's perfectly obvious that that Pierce girl is malevolent by nature.'

Julius looked up from the spelling book he was pretending to study.

'Are you talking about Tulip?'

Mrs Pettifer couldn't order Miss Ferguson to be quiet. Instead, she sent Julius out of the lounge.

'Off you go, dear. I'm sure you can't be doing your homework properly here.'

Julius trailed away, probably glad of the excuse to give up on his spellings. I expect Mrs Pettifer glanced round to check I wasn't listening, either. But I was well hidden. So by the time that Mum came over to have a few words with them before dinner, the three had started up again.

'I was just telling Mrs Pettifer,' said Miss Ferguson, 'that part of the problem for children today is that they hear far too many people like herself telling them they understand all their problems, and not enough like me stating quite openly that some of their behaviour is downright evil.'

Old Mr Hearns had kept dead quiet up till then. He'd probably been hoping that this discussion would die away, and he'd be asked to play the piano, as usual. But now he got irritated, and spoke up.

'Oh, I see! They're bad seeds, are they? Spawn of the devil?'

She missed his sarcasm entirely.

'That's right!' she said. 'And when I was a girl, these things were made perfectly clear to us. We even had to learn a little poem. "Satan is glad when I am bad."'

'Oh, I know that one!'

This was Mr Scott Henderson, who winked at me as he strolled in behind George, who was carrying a tray of drinks from the bar. Rumbled, I stepped out from behind the pillar. But no one noticed me. They were still busy looking at Mr Scott Henderson, who had clasped his hands together, and started declaiming:

'"Satan is glad
When I am bad
And hopes that I
With him shall lie
In fire and chains
And awful pains."'

'Hardly a *poem*,' Mr Hearns muttered critically. But Mum took the chance to stop the argument in its tracks by starting a small storm of clapping. Mr Scott Henderson took a bow. And after a 'please break it up' eye-signal from Mum, George made a point of giving everyone the wrong drinks. In the confusion that followed, Mum leaned over the arm of Mr Hearns's chair, and said softly:

'I think a tune would be nice now, don't you?'

Gratefully, he rose and launched into what I've often heard Mum call 'that awful stale medley of his'. Mum kept the smile fixed on her face, and nodded to the music. And she was still determinedly humming 'Bye-Bye Blackbird' when the grandfather clock took to striking its arthritic half hour, and all of them finally prised themselves out of their armchairs and off their sofas, and wandered across the lobby, into the dining room.

Mum's bright look crumpled like a dead balloon. Leaning her head against the chair back, she closed her eyes. I thought she might call me over to talk about the visit from the police, and what I'd said about Tulip's father. But, within seconds, the telephone outside was ringing again. She waited and waited. And when it was obvious that none of the staff was close enough to take it, she sighed and levered herself to her feet.

A few moments later, she was gone.

5

She wouldn't let the guests get into fights. But upstairs she and Dad went at it hammer and tongs.

'Miss Ferguson's quite right. Tulip is downright *evil*.'

'I can't believe I'm hearing you right, Emma. You know those old biddies down there are light years from knowing the first thing about children. No one is born evil. No one. And especially not Tulip.'

Mum turned away to tip stale flower water in the sink, and run in fresh.

'I don't know how else you'd explain something so horrible.'

'Oh, don't be so silly. You know as well as I do that Tulip's had such a rotten start in life that it's hardly a surprise she's insensitive to other people's feelings.'

'There's a bit more to this than being insensitive!' snapped Mum, slamming the vase back on the table.

He reached out to steady it.

'You know what I mean. To really know right from wrong you need a certain emotional sympathy. And you only learn that from being treated properly yourself.'

'Tulip's not stupid. Tulip knows the rules.'

'Why should she think rules matter? Her father's are vindictive and wilful, and sometimes it must seem to her that, whatever she does, she gets punished. So why should she bother about rules?'

I had to keep myself from turning round. I'd no idea, before this argument, that they knew so much about Tulip.

'Why should she bother? Because she's bright enough to see that if enough people like her go round doing exactly what they want, *everyone's* miserable.'

'If you've been brought up as if your feelings don't matter, you probably assume other people's don't matter much either.'

In the corner, Julius's computer game chattered to its climax. Mum's voice rose above it.

'Don't kid yourself! Tulip knows perfectly well how much other people's feelings matter. And that's exactly why she does these things. That's the amusement she gets from them. Why else would she do it?'

Dad couldn't think of an answer. He just shrugged. And then, reluctant to give up his defence of Tulip, he said:

'Well, you only have to pick up a paper to read about kids a lot younger doing worse.'

To prove his point, he read Mum a paragraph from the *Chronicle* lying on the table about the murder of a boy in Elvenwater where the police were quite sure that the killer was no older than the victim. I don't remember the details. Something to do with footprints, and a squabble overheard by somebody pegging out washing, and too many people noticing two young people going down the path, only one coming back. I do remember the police were certain. The one they were looking for was even younger than me.

Mum listened, but she wouldn't budge.

'Children with violent tempers, I can understand,' she said. 'Even children with too few brains to realize how dangerous a game is getting. But Tulip's visits to the Brackenburys are out of another box entirely. They're not just bad. They're different. And that's what evil is. Something *different*.'

'There's no such thing as evil. You know that.'

And round and round they went, round and round, while I leaned over Julius's shoulder, and pretended to be absorbed in his fast-rising score. Mum had barely begun on the vase on the side table before Dad was arguing with her again.

'Look, Emma. Even professionals come across the odd child they just can't stand. The child they can't help thinking is deeply, deeply mean inside. And then what usually happens is that they meet the parents. And they begin to think, "Poor little brute. No wonder the child's such a horror." '

'Oh, right!' scoffed Mum. 'Then I've got a brilliant idea. Why don't you take Mr and Mrs Pierce round to meet Mrs Brackenbury? Then she can start feeling sorry for Tulip.'

That shut Dad up.

'*See?*' Mum said, and walked past him into the bathroom, carrying the misting spray. She made a point of letting the door close behind her.

The buzzer from downstairs rang twice.

Dad pushed himself up from the table. Seeing me watching, he pushed the newspaper over the table towards me, and said darkly:

'Good thing that Tulip has an alibi!'

It was a joke. But what he didn't know was that, after the paper came earlier, I'd spent a good half hour kneeling on the chest in the passage, scouring the map for Elvenwater, checking the scale, and doing the calculation over and over, till I was absolutely sure.

6

And it wasn't the first time, either. Ever since the blaze at the chicken farm, I'd scoured the evening paper every night. As I came in from school, Dad would lift his head from the computer, or turn from the rack of numbered room keys.

'Be an angel, Natalie. Take round the papers.'

I'd scoop the pile of *Chronicles* into my arms. And round I'd go. Slap, slap. One on every second sofa. Slap. Three on the menu table. Two in the bar. Two in the coffee room. All the rest in the lounge.

Except for the one I took up to my bedroom. I read the whole thing. Thefts. Beatings. Vandalism. I'd dutifully turn each page. **FIRE INJURES HOMELESS MAN.** The usual thing. They must print stories like it ten times a week. A garbled account from someone passing by of how he smelled the smoke and saw the flames. And, just above, a picture of a burnt-out shed. I'd try to tell myself a drunk tramp nearly died in a fire, and that was that. Just because Tulip lit fires, it didn't follow that she started this one.

But still she'd be my chief suspect. Sometimes I'd be so convinced that it was her, I'd have to stop and read the report again. Only then would I see the words 'Wednesday lunchtime' and remind myself that I'd seen her flouncing into detention at that time. 'The suspect was male,' I'd notice on second reading. 'The suspect is six feet tall.'

And who were they, anyway, these people who filled up the pages of the *Chronicle*, night after night? Were they all like Tulip, living life as one game after another? Tire of one, and move on to another even harder and more dangerous? They couldn't all have fathers as vile and bullying as Mr Pierce, and mothers too feeble to protect them. Surely there weren't that many horrid people in the world. And, if there were, I wasn't sure I wanted to go on buses any more, or walk down streets, for fear of bumping into them.

Dad found me in the passage once too often.

'Quite the little cartographer,' he said as he passed.

'What?'

'Maps,' he called over his shoulder. 'Each time I see you these days, you're kneeling on that chest, studying the map.'

'I was just checking something.'

Suddenly he stopped, and put the television he was carrying down on the floor.

'Room 302,' he said. 'Don't let me forget.' Then he sat on the chest beside me and pushed my hair out of my eyes.

'Is something worrying you, Natalie? Is there anything wrong?'

Everyone has choices. I'd shied away from him time and again because, close to Tulip, I didn't need him. Tulip's touch was enough. But now she wasn't there, I realized I'd been hiding from both my parents. I'd used the fact that they were busy, and Mum was so wrapped up in Julius, to slip away from them and keep them off me. And it had worked. If you're a good girl, and dress neatly, and do your homework, no one will even notice you. You can leave a pretend person in your place to say 'Good morning', and pass the beans, and carry the dishes to the hatch. If they're not looking, then they'll never know.

Or you can raise a hand to save yourself. Make sure they see you.

'I was just looking at the map,' I said. 'To work out if it could be Tulip who stabbed that old lady on Thursday in Bridleford.'

He turned to stare.

'What?'

I kept my voice steady.

'But that lady was stabbed and robbed at three o'clock, the police say. And we didn't finish with the school photo till after two-thirty. And Bridleford's miles away.' I showed him, to scale, with my fingers. 'And Tulip has no bike. So I reckon Tulip has an alibi.'

He was still staring.

'Is this what you've been doing each time I've seen you on this trunk?'

I nodded.

He shook his head in amazement.

'But why on earth would you think it was Tulip?'

'Well, tell me,' I said. 'Who are these people, if they're not people like her?'

'Listen,' he said. 'This is ridiculous. I know Tulip's turning into a bit of a bad lot, but –'

I interrupted him.

'You were around at lunch. You heard Mrs Pettifer telling everyone what the policeman told his wife.'

Dad looked irritated.

'Gossip! Rubbishy gossip! These old biddies should keep their mouths shut.'

But I knew he knew better.

' "It isn't a home," he told her. "That house is just a cold shell keeping the rain off three people. I was there half an hour," he said. "And the only real life in there was that great big dog barking." '

Dad sighed.

'Oh, dear. Poor Tulip.'

That wasn't going to wash. I turned on him accusingly.

'And you knew that. You've known it years and years. That's why you never let me go round there, even at the start. Even back then I heard you telling Mum it was –' I imitated his stern voice – ' "No fit place for a child." '

'Well, then,' he said rather smugly. 'I was right.'

'But *Tulip* was a child, wasn't she? If you were so sure I shouldn't have been there, then Tulip shouldn't have been there, either.'

'Natalie, people can't go round snatching children and giving them other homes just because their parents are awful.'

'She shouldn't have been left,' I said stubbornly.

He tried to take my hand.

'You really mustn't think that nobody tried. I know for a fact we weren't the only ones to make a few warning phone calls. And both schools were always well aware of Tulip's background. The Pierces have had social workers round there time and again.'

So everybody was in on it! Everyone knew!

'So what was the matter?' I asked sarcastically. 'Wasn't it bad enough?'

He rose to his feet and looked down at me.

'No,' he said evenly after a moment. 'It wasn't bad enough. And I'm afraid that life's a bit like that, Natalie. It has to be a whole lot worse than bad to count as unbearable. And, till it gets to that point, people are on their own.'

I was disgusted. Utterly disgusted.

'They've got to stick up for themselves, have they?' I said scornfully. 'Manage on their own?'

He paused. Then,

'Why not?' His voice was still even. 'You've heard Mrs Pettifer say it often enough. "Every saint has a past. Every sinner has a future." And you've even managed it yourself. Look at you. No more warnings on your report cards. No more lost hours after school. Better marks. Better habits. You've let down Tulip and you've saved yourself.'

I wanted to scream at him, 'Yes, but I'm not like you, am I? I've got no power to change things. You lot *have*.'

But what would have been the point? He couldn't afford to believe me. None of them could. That way, they'd have to feel as guilty as me.

So I didn't say anything. I just nodded at the television he'd left on the floor. 'Don't forget,' I said. 'You're going to Room 302.'

'Oh, right.'

He took the hint then, and he walked away.

7

And after that, I put Tulip Pierce out of my mind, and got on with my own life. This time I did it properly. I spent my break-times in the library, gradually daring to take a seat nearer and nearer one of the small groups of girls who sat together, till one day Glenys asked if she could borrow my red felt tipped pen, and Anna told me that she liked my hair.

And from then on, I joined them in the lunch queue every day, and walked to the bus stop with Glenys. A week or so later, when she was chatting about the party she was planning at the weekend, she asked me, 'Why don't you come too?'

And I was in at last.

I still saw Tulip in the corridors, on days she came. And, like the rest of them, I took an interest in her foul-tempered brushes with the staff, and all her defiant rebellions.

'Did you hear what she called Mrs Minniver? Everyone's saying she'll be asked to leave.'

'My dad heard that she'd been reported to the police for slashing the bus seats.'

'It wasn't bus seats. It was theft.'

Tulip stormed up the staircases, and in and out of rooms, snarling at everyone.

'Move out of the way, idiot!'

And most of them did. She made almost everyone nervous. I think they all thought that someone the staff could barely pretend to control was far too dangerous even to stand near. The trouble she got in, instead of curbing her, seemed to make her worse. She became more and more insolent, almost insanely cocksure. Indifferent to threats and warnings, even to punishment, she took her continual suspensions in her stride. We'd see her swaggering out between the gates at all hours of the day, and not be able to begin to guess whether she'd been sent home officially, or just decided it was time to go.

But, as her reputatuion grew, so did mine. In March, I passed all my exams so well I was commended. Miss Fowler called in my parents and told them she was moving me into a different stream.

'It will be hard,' she said. 'But Natalie is doing so well, I'm sure she'll manage.'

And I did. Easily. Somehow, the harder I worked, the more I enjoyed it. And when, at the end of the school year,

I won three of the prizes and had to walk across the stage in front of everyone to take my books and shake Miss Fowler's hand, I realized Tulip and I had now reached equal distinction in our separate ways. Everyone knew me for an excellent pupil. And everyone knew her for a bad lot.

And then I bumped into her in the cloakroom.

'Move over, stupid!' she snapped at me, pushing past.

Perhaps she'd called me that once too often when we were younger. Or maybe, still carrying my brand-new prizes, I wasn't ready to be insulted any more.

Anyhow, stupid I was. Deliberately, quite deliberately, I let my eyes slide off her face, down her stained pullover to her puckered skirt.

And wrinkled my nose.

One look in her eyes, and I knew I'd gone far too far.

'Oh, so we're playing games again, are we?'

Hastily, I tried to backtrack.

'I don't know what you mean.'

She just ignored me.

'We haven't played one for ages, have we, Natalie? What do you feel like? *Hogs in a Tunnel*? *Havoc*? *Road of Bones*? How about *Watch the Skies*? You always enjoyed that.'

I'd never realized eyes could go so hard. Suddenly I felt sick with fright.

'Leave me alone, Tulip!'

She made her eyes go wide.

'That's not very nice, is it? After all, you were the one to start.'

'I haven't started anything.'

'Yes, you have. You just began with *Stinking Mackerel*. I saw you.'

Nobody knows you like your old best friend. There was no point in saying anything. I just made for the door.

'That's agreed, is it?' she called after me. 'Now it's my turn to choose.'

I pretended I wasn't listening. Tugging the swing doors to make them close faster behind me, I hurried down the long corridor to get away. When, at the corner, I glanced back, she wasn't behind me. But that wasn't any comfort. After all, she had no need to follow me herself. Her menacing little words were doing that.

I rushed into the safety of my next class, and took my seat, my heart thumping. Nobody looked my way. Nobody noticed. But I sat there in terror. I knew Tulip. And, deep inside, not only did I know that she'd not rest till she'd won the very last game of all. I also knew exactly which of them she'd choose.

8

The next few days, I felt like that poor trembling rabbit in Tulip's clutch, waiting for something to happen. But one week turned into two, then three, and Tulip never even glanced my way. And then, at the end of the next week, the holidays started.

Time and again, that summer, I checked with Julius.

'You haven't seen Tulip hanging around anywhere, have you?'

He'd look up from whatever he was doing.

'Tulip? No. Why? Is she coming round?'

'I don't think so. But if you see her, will you let me know?'

I'd try not to sound worried, and maybe that was a mistake. Because once, when I asked him, I got a different answer.

'I thought I saw her a couple of days ago, by the old garages. But when I called her, she just disappeared.'

'Next time, tell me straight away, will you?'

'If you like.'

I searched the garages, but found nothing. And, looking back, I'm not surprised. Tulip was cleverer than that. The days went by. Dad started paying me for little jobs, and Mum needed help in the office, so I was kept busy. Glenys came over once or twice, and I went to her house. And gradually I let myself believe that all Tulip had in mind that day was making me nervous. She knew exactly how faint-hearted I could be. What could be smarter than leaving me to worry, week after week, about something she'd long forgotten?

And so I let myself stop fretting. There was so much to do. When school term began again after the summer, I had a whole lot more work and netball practice twice a week. I got a part in the school play, and what with the flurry of extra rehearsals after half term, before I could believe it, Christmas was on its way again.

'Are you inviting Glenys?'

'No,' I said. 'She's off to her dad's house.'

'How about Anna, then?'

'She says her mum would have a fit if she went to someone else for Christmas.'

Dad shrugged.

'Makes sense. I wouldn't like it if you were away.'

So I was there. There in my new green skirt through all the sherries and the canapés. There through Mr Hearns's Christmas medley on the piano. There through the charity raffle.

And there through the carols, as usual, with Julius bravely singing the first verse of *Once in Royal David's City* all alone, and Mrs Scott Henderson chiming in on every last verse with her ghastly descants, and Mr Hearns faltering even more than usual because he'd mislaid his glasses. The guests sang out, their faces winking from brightness to shadow as, through the french windows, the coloured lights along the terraces blinked on and off, on and off, over and over.

Oh, clever, clever Tulip! To pick the one evening everyone's in the same room, and all the kitchen staff who haven't managed to persuade Dad they're not needed are running round in circles, or peering into special soups, or diving into ovens to check on yet another difficult dish. Clever, clever Tulip, to pick the only night no one's around to see a small dark figure pouring petrol, and paraffin, and God knows what else, on all the sills and lintels, all the doors and benches, railings and signs, everything wooden round an old hotel.

And clever Tulip, to give herself a good head start. To choose the night when no one is going to notice, till it's far too late, that the sherry-flushed faces in the firelight are blinking pinker and brighter, pinker and brighter.

'Fire! Fire! Outside on the verandah! *Fire!*'

Alarms went off as the first flames broke through. The sprinkler system Dad put in the year we came spun into action at once. Everyone did the right thing. Nobody panicked. The guests, as Mum said afterwards, were 'Marvellous! Marvellous!' They gathered on the lawns, and ticked each other off on lists as though they'd been in fires all their lives. No one sneaked back inside to fetch their jewellery. No one played daft heroics for the cat. And though Cedric had to be dragged away from the oven in which his *Boeufs en Croute* were crisping up nicely, all the kitchen staff switched off their grills and their gas jets in an orderly fashion, and left immediately through the nearest doors.

So by the time the first of Tulip's carefully primed explosions shattered the glass in the conservatory, everyone was safely out, watching the flames take hold. And if she hadn't thought to dig away the leaf mould of a hundred years to drag closed the giant iron gates at the bottom of the drive (and loop them round with so many chains and padlocks that the firemen believed her when she called out to them, 'No! Not these gates! The other ones. Round there!'), then the first fire engine wouldn't have got bogged down in the muddy lane leading to their farm, and the second one would have broken in just that much quicker.

And so the Palace burned. Julius and I stood side by side to watch. His face flared in the fire's dancing light as one dark framed window after another burst into a fierce glow.

He turned to me, his cheeks burning as much with excitement as the reflection of the flames.

'Was it Tulip?'

My face was probably as flushed as his as I began the long, long lie.

'Now how on earth should *I* know?'

Cheerfully, he turned back to the blaze to watch the firemen send their huge coils of water snaking over the parapets. Like Tulip's stolen gold necklace hurled in the rubbish drum all that time ago, they slithered into the building's giant shell, and vanished instantly. I wondered, was she watching too? How did it feel, to see the only place she ever loved go up in flames? Inside, the dimpled copper bar top she used to stroke was buckling and melting. The glorious curving banisters she trailed her fingers up a million times were twisting to ugly shapes as they charred. Did she *care*? Was she hidden up somewhere in a tree behind us, just like one more roosting peacock, crying her eyes out? Or had she simply laughed, and run off home for yet another beating for being late?

Dad came up behind, and rested his hands on our shoulders. He couldn't say a word. He just stood there and watched. And so did Mum. We stood in silence as the Palace gradually gave up the fight, and out of the deafening hissing and spitting and crackling and roaring, the silent billows of smoke curled away in defeat over the huge dark spinney where Tulip had crept to hide her dangerous little toys week after week, till she was ready to play the very last, very worst, game of all.

9

So now we're off. Tomorrow we leave for Nettle Underwood. The Starbuck Arms. Dad's pretty cheerful about it. Sometimes you'd think that Tulip had done him a favour.

'These grand old buildings like the Palace have had their day,' he keeps telling everyone. 'Too many planning rules. Hotels that size can't stay afloat with just a few loyal regulars and passing tourists. These days you really have to be up-to-date. Leisure centres. Swimming pools. A proper dance floor. Lifts to every level. They've got all those at the Starbuck.'

Mum's come to terms with losing so many things. She had a weep about some photographs that were ruined (mostly because they were ones of Julius, I expect). And there were a couple of phone calls with the insurance people that left her shaking with rage. But yesterday she looked round the mess and clutter in the room where she's dumped all we have left, and said to me,

'Nothing worth dusting. Nothing worth bothering about. Come for a walk with me, Natalie. Let's go and have coffee together in the village.'

And no one there minds much. Drinks at the hotel were always too expensive for most of the people round here. And the company's selling the site to someone who wants to build nice modern houses. So they don't mind, either. They're not blaming Dad. After all, he's never made a serious mistake before. And though an accidental fire should have been stopped at the outset, everyone's agreed that arson's another matter.

I worried terribly about Julius. But it turns out he doesn't care a hoot. He won't say anything in front of them, but to me he's admitted it. He enjoyed the fire. 'Brilliant!' he calls it. He's become famous at school, describing it over and over. And though we're leaving now, he says he never wanted to move on to Talbot Harries anyway. He's glad he's going to another school.

And so am I. Everyone needs the chance to start again. Though I was doing pretty well, it seems. I know because on Friday, Miss Fowler called me in to show me the report she's sending on to Nettle Underwood. 'After a period of confusion, Natalie Barnes has made a prodigious effort to find herself. She should go on to better and better things, and we all wish her well.' I told Glenys we were leaving, and promised her that I'd write every week. But, if I'm honest, I'll miss her less than the stone boy in the lily pond. She's never been a close friend.

Not like Tulip.

I don't think I'll be seeing her again. Her name comes up the whole time, of course, what with the gossip about the police enquiry, and the probation officer's report. Mum calls her 'That witch Tulip!' and Dad says 'Nonsense, Emma!' every time. But I can't help but think that being a real witch would have been better for her. At least that way she'd have a little power. Tulip's got nothing now. Yesterday, when we were packing, Julius asked me,

'If you could rub Tulip out of your past life, would you do it?'

And I had to shake my head. I can't regret the times we had together. Sometimes I worry I won't have times like that again, that there will be no lit nights, no incandescent days. But I know it's not true. There can be colour in a million ways. I know I'll find it on my own.

I have strange dreams about her. Sometimes the two of us are sitting cross-legged in one of the outhouses behind her farm, stirring a liquid we call 'flame-water', or crawling on our bellies through an orchard, trying to set fire to the flowers. But mostly, when I dream, Tulip and I are back in our first school, giggling and being silly, or lying on our backs behind the parapet, our bare arms touching, playing *Watch the Skies*.

I think about the day that Dad and I first saw her in that field of corn, and try to tell myself it was already too late. There's no particular moment when someone goes to the bad. Each horrible thing that happens makes a difference, and there had probably been too many of those already in Tulip's life.

But I can't convince myself. Yes, now I know that even back then, Tulip was going off to drown that poor kitten. But Dad was no older the day he pushed his grandfather's tortoise under the bush and left it there to die. You could say that Tulip was braver and kinder. And people aren't locked doors. You can get through to them if you want.

But no one did. No one reached out a hand to Tulip. Nobody tried to touch her. I hear them whispering and they sicken me. 'Bus seats!' grumbles Mrs Bodell. 'Locker doors!' complain the teachers. 'Chicken sheds!' say the farmers. 'Greenhouses! Dustbins!' moan the neighbours. And Mum says, 'A lovely old hotel!'

But what about Tulip?

I shall feel sorry for Tulip all my life.

And guilty, too.

Guilty.

REBEL STORIES

THE ORIGINALS

REBEL: **Pony Boy Curtis**, *Greaser*

SKILL: *Writing (he penned* THE ORIGINAL *teenage rebel story)*

CAUSE: *Protecting his friend after a fight with rival gang, the Socs, leads to a fatal knifing*

S.E. Hinton
The Outsiders

REBEL: **Sipho**, *a young South African runaway*

SKILL: *Bravery*

CAUSE: *Surviving on the cut-throat streets of post-apartheid South Africa*

NO TURNING BACK
Beverley Naidoo

REBEL: **Kino**, *a Mexican pearl diver and dedicated father*

SKILL: *Possesses a precious pearl that is coveted by all*

CAUSE: *Overcoming the prejudice that endangers his son's life*

THE PEARL
JOHN STEINBECK

Whose side are you on?   **#OriginalYA**

REBEL: **Jerry Renault**, *Newcomer at Trinity College*

SKILLS: Resilience and determination

CAUSE: *To expose the corrupt leader of the Vigils*

REBEL: **Rusty**, *orphan*

SKILL: Perseverance

CAUSE: *To escape from his strict guardian and find freedom*

REBEL: **Mark**, *tough punk*

SKILLS: Stealing cars and fighting

CAUSE: *To get even*

REBEL: **Tulip**, *loner*

SKILLS: bizarre games

CAUSE: *To befriend and destroy*

THE ORIGINALS
Iconic • Outspoken • First

FOR THINKERS

- [ ] **Dear Nobody**
  Berlie Doherty

- [ ] **Buddy**
  Nigel Hinton

- [ ] **The Red Pony**
  John Steinbeck

- [ ] **The Wave**
  Morton Rhue

FOR LOVERS

- [ ] **I Capture the Castle**
  Dodie Smith

- [ ] **Across the Barricades**
  Joan Lingard

- [ ] **UnArranged Marriage**
  Bali Rai

- [ ] **Postcards from No Man's Land**
  Aidan Chambers

FOR REBELS

- [ ] **The Outsiders**
  S. E. Hinton

- [ ] **The Pearl**
  John Steinbeck

- [ ] **No Turning Back**
  Reverley Naidoo

- [ ] **Alanna**
  Tamora Pierce

FOR SURVIVORS

- [ ] **Z for Zachariah**
  Richard C. O'Brien

- [ ] **After the First Death**
  Robert Cormier

- [ ] **Stone Cold**
  Robert Swindells

- [ ] **The Endless Steppe**
  Esther Hautzig

What are you reading? Tell **@penguinplatform #OriginalYA**